The Prince Who Lost his Pants

By D. F. Zaman

Copyright ©2023 *D. F. Zaman*

This book is dedicated to my mother.

Special thanks to Vahije Golmazari, cover illustrator.

Chapter One - Two Princes

Prince David was extraordinary. He was kind, caring and honest with a face that reflected his personality. His eyes were a deep, dazzling blue, as blue as the deepest ocean on a clear sunny day. His hair was so dark, it was almost black. You might say that black hair and blue eyes are an unusual combination on a person but then, David was a very rare and unusual young man.

"What made him so rare?" you might ask. Well, David was rare because he was incredibly insightful for a person of his age. Being insightful is a gift. It is the ability to get to the heart of things, to see and understand things that others don't understand.

In other words, David was special. He was a thinking man, and this was a good thing for a prince because every good ruler needs to think carefully so that he makes the right decision for his people every time.

Being thoughtful wasn't David's only gift though. When David was at school, his teacher wrote in his school report that:

"The most striking thing about David is his empathy for others,"

She wasn't wrong because, as well as being a deep thinker, David was also a man of deep feeling. He was so sensitive he could feel what other people were feeling- their pain, their suffering, their joy, their sorrow.

His genuine empathy for his people made him incredibly popular.

A more popular prince could not be found anywhere in the world. David was mobbed everywhere he went. Young girls kept his picture in their room. Young boys dreamt of growing up to be just like him and everyone had high hopes for the handsome, kind, clever young man who had won their hearts and minds.

But there was a problem. David wasn't the only prince in the palace. David had a cousin who was the exact opposite of all that David was.

While David was empathetic, Septicus was boorish. While David was caring, Septic was only ever concerned about himself, no one else.

Where David felt sympathy and kindness towards the weak and the less fortunate, Septicus felt only contempt.

In fact, Septicus liked to have people who were weaker and poorer than him because it made him feel special and strong because unlike David, Septicus was not wise. He did not understand that trampling on the weak was not a sign of strength but of cowardice, the sign of a bully, a weak personality who picks on people who cannot fight back.

The differences between the two princes were clear from the start. As boys, while Septicus took great delight in cruelly tearing the wings off pretty, little butterflies and ladybirds, David, full of pity for the weak, defenceless little creatures, would try to glue them back on again! Superglue never lasted long in the palace when David was around!

While Septicus trampled the pretty flowers in the garden, David planted new ones. While Septicus left rubbish lying around everywhere, expecting people to clear his mess up for him, David cleared up after himself. The servants had enough work to do as it was. He didn't want to add to their burdens.

As the children grew into teenagers, not surprisingly, David became the more popular of the two, and seeing David's popularity, Septicus seethed inside. The last straw came one day when Septicus's mother said to him, *"Look at David. Look at how charming he is. Look how everybody loves him."*

Septicus's resentment for David boiled over into hate, hatred of his *"goody two shoes, annoying, irritating," cousin, David."* As if David hadn't annoyed him enough, to add insult to injury, now, even his own mother admired David more than she admired him! This was too much. This was humiliating. Something had to be done!

Septicus decided to be charming just like his cousin David to make everyone think that he was good like David. He learned to walk like David, talk like David, charm the birds off the trees like David and soon, people began to warm to him just as they had warmed to David.

Comparisons were made between Septicus and David about how similar they were, how charming they were but little did the people know that unfortunately, surface charm was where the similarity ended because unlike David, Septicus had a cold and arrogant heart.

Even though he was charming and smooth on the outside, on the inside, he was still his spiteful and hateful self, jealous of his cousin who would one day become king.

"It can't be right for that self-righteous do-gooder to be king," thought Septicus petulantly. *"I am the strongest. I am the toughest. I am the handsomest. I am the one who can beat anyone to a pulp. A king needs to be tough and rule with a rod of iron. I am the one who ought to be king!"*

It was true that Septicus was a handsome man and very impressive to look at. He was tall, broad and very strong with masses of rich golden hair and a strong, handsome face but his eyes were very different to David's.

Whereas David's eyes were warm, gentle and kind, Septicus's eyes were cold and hard and could give a look that could chill a person to the very bone for its coldness.

Whereas David's eyes were a warm, turquoise, "sea on a sunny day" blue, Septicus's eyes were a cold, icy, glacial blue that matched his cold, icy, glacial heart.

Also, Septicus was a very vain man. His mirror was his best friend. Many were the times when he would stand in front of the mirror, gazing adoringly at his own image for hours, blowing kisses to himself.

"My, my, you're such a glorious hunk of a man Septicus. Damn you! Septicus, you handsome devil!" he would mutter quietly to himself as he flirted with himself shamelessly in the mirror. *"Watch out ladies, here I come!"* he would whisper under his breath as he would admire the arch of his eyebrow for the hundredth time !

I suppose you could say that Septicus was just a little bit in love with himself!

A wise person once said that you can tell a good person from a bad person from the way they treat their enemies. Even a horrible person can be nice to their friends but only a good person can be honest about their enemies.

David would never tell a malicious lie about anyone as he knew that this was a low thing to do. It was cheating and it was being unfair whereas Septicus didn't care about being fair. He just cared about winning. He would say anything and do anything in order to win a fight. He would poke you in the shins, trip you up, tell a horrible lie or throw dirt in your eye. There was nothing he wouldn't do.

Being decent and fair didn't matter to Septicus at all. Winning was the only thing that mattered to him! He did not treat people as people but as pawns in a chess game that he had to win!

Septicus was not a good person and so for all his surface charm, he was never going to be a patch on his cousin David because unlike Septicus, David was the only one who was good enough to be a king, so it was just as well that he was the first in line to the throne after his father, King Nigel, the twenty second!

Now, everyone knows that a king must have a queen so when David reached the ripe old age of twenty one and had finished his Environmental Studies degree at university, his father and mother decided that it was time for him to find a bride.

King Nigel and Queen Seraphina searched worldwide for a suitable bride for their precious prince. For four whole years, Prince David was forced to attend innumerable princes' balls in dozens of countries including far flung places like Azerbaijan, Kazakhstan and Turkmenistan (look them up- they're in the atlas of the world) as well as the usual European countries of France, Spain, Italy, Iceland and so on.

Many were the evenings when he was forced to foxtrot with a fine Finnish princess or salsa with a stunning Spanish princess at yet another princes' ball but somehow, for some reason, no matter how many adorable, incredible beauties he met, he never seemed to manage to fall in love with anyone.

After David had been introduced to dozens of beautiful princesses from the world over, his parents began to worry.

"What's wrong with the boy?" asked his father.

"Is he ill?" asked Queen Seraphina. *"Surely, he should have fallen in love with someone by now! Oh, where did we go wrong?"* wailed the queen. *"What are we going to do?"*

The king and the queen fell into despair. David was King Nigel's one and only son and heir and King Nigel and the queen were worried. They didn't understand what was wrong with the boy. He was usually so good at everything so why was he so slow at falling in love?

To be fair, David didn't understand it either. He knew that these princesses were very beautiful and that by rights, he should be in love with at least one of them by now but no matter how nice they were or how charmingly they danced or how beautiful they looked, he just couldn't let them into his heart! Why? That was the gazillion dollar question. He just didn't know!

David sought advice from his childhood friend, Amelia. Amelia was the daughter of one of the palace gardeners and David had known her since she was a tiny tot. Then, when they had found themselves at the same university together for three years, their childhood friendship had blossomed further. David thought it would be useful to get some advice from a girl on such matters so, he decided to call her up and ask her what to do.

Now, Amelia had secretly loved the prince since they were children, but she thought that the king and queen would not approve of him marrying a gardener's daughter no matter how bright or pretty or good and kind she was, so she said nothing to the prince.

When David came to see her after months of being apart, doing the princes ball circuit, she was secretly thrilled although she did her best not to let it show. Amelia was a strong and private young lady who kept her feelings to herself ... most of the time.

"Davey! It's so good to see you after all this time!" she exclaimed as she gave him a big, friendly hug. *"You have to tell me all your news. I want to hear absolutely everything,"* so David did just that. He told her everything!

He told her about the princess of Spain with her beautiful dark eyes, her beautiful, glossy, coffee-coloured curls and her beautiful, rich, resonant singing voice.

He told her about the Icelandic princess with her quick wit, her boisterous laugh, her amazing charm and her ability to turn cartwheels at 35 miles an hour!

He told her about the princess of Azerbaijan with her passionate poetry, her funky dance moves and her pretty heart-shaped face with the pretty chin that tapered to a point!

"All these princesses were beautiful and accomplished," he groaned, *"but no matter how brilliant they were, none of them were right for me. Try as I might, I couldn't fall in love with any of them and I don't know why! What is wrong with me Amelia?"* he asked, desperate for an answer. *"What should I do?"*

Amelia chewed her lip thoughtfully. She thought long and hard. This was a tough one. She had that thoughtful look on her face she usually had when she was concentrating hard on something, a look that David had come to know and love over all the years that they had known each other.

"Hmm...." she said at length. *"David, you've got a loving and a good heart. I know that. Everybody knows that, so if you're not able to let any of these amazing girls into your heart, then, could it be........"* She hesitated as if unsure.

"Go on," urged David. *"Tell me what you think. Be honest with me."*

"Well, could it be David that you've already got someone in your heart so there's no room for anyone else? Could it be perhaps that you're already in love with someone and you just don't know it..... yet?"

David considered for a moment. Although he was usually an insightful person, he was stumped by this one because clever though he was, everyone knows that when it comes to love, even the wisest of people can be fools. David sighed deeply and now, it was his turn to look thoughtful.

Amelia smiled to herself when she saw that look. That was the look that she had seen on David's face when she was six years old and had come running down the garden path to her grandfather, tears pouring down her face after Septicus had pushed her into a rosebush and she'd cut her finger on a thorn. David, who had been close by at the time, had rushed over and helped to bandage up the wounds with a little bit of help from her grandfather. That was the look that she had seen on his face as he had carefully and gently covered the scratches on her arms with plasters and helped her to dry her tears. She knew him so well.

"Amelia, if I were in love, wouldn't I know? Wouldn't it be obvious? I mean - how can I be in love and not know it? Surely, I would feel something."

"Well, I wouldn't worry too much Davey. You've got plenty of time yet," was Amelia's comforting reply, *"It'll be another five years before you're thirty and over the hill and you'll have to marry the first girl who comes along!"*

David laughed. That was what he loved about Amelia. She could always make him laugh no matter what, even when he felt as if the sky was crashing down on him. She always knew what to say to make him see the funny side of things. No matter how much time they spent apart, it was as if it had been no time at all. She was a true and trusted confidante and friend.

"I've really missed you Amelia," he said, *"What would I ever do without you?"*

"Well, you'll never be without me silly," she reassured him, *"because I'm always going to be around for you. You are never going to be without me. Friends forever, remember?"*

David smiled fondly when she said this. This was something they had promised each other when they had parted just before he was sent off to boarding school when he was eleven.

Of course, he remembered!

Chapter Two - Septicus the Sneak

Meanwhile, as David and Amelia had been talking, someone had been listening, someone very nasty and someone very nosy because in addition to being a liar and a cheat, Septicus was also a habitual eavesdropper who made it his business to know everything about everyone because you never knew when something you overheard might come in handy.

Septicus remembered the time when he had found out that the headmaster at his old school wore frilly pink underpants to school. He chuckled a low, deep, throaty malevolent chuckle as he remembered the fun that he had had with that one!

He had made the headmaster sign him off cookery and music lessons every week for the next five years! After all, everyone knew that cookery was for GIRLS!

Then, there was the time when he had found out that the scullery maid had been kissing the butler in the pantry. He had had them fired over that one! Oh! The look of terror in their eyes when he had found out!

Oh! The power! He loved the feeling of power he got when he saw the look of terror in people's eyes, the fear, the trembling when he put them in their place! He loved showing people who was in charge!

Now, Septicus's hatred of David had made him desperate to find something shocking about David so he had spent hours sneakily eavesdropping on David's private conversations, hoping to find some scandalous information he could use against him but he had found nothing, absolutely nothing. It was disappointing.

David and that gardener girl Amelia's conversations were so totally proper and boring. It was enough to send a person to sleep. In fact, wait for it, he could already feel a massive yawn coming on! Oh, there it was "YAWWN!"

"Those two are such a boring pair of goody two shoes," he thought malevolently. *"You can listen for hours and hours to their dreary conversations and never get any dirt on them."*

Now, by dirt Septic didn't mean the kind of dirt that you get on a football pitch when it rains or the dirt that you get in a dustpan. He meant information about things that people had done, sinister or terrible things that they were ashamed of like..... putting peas up someone's nose when they were sleeping or picking their ears and making candles out of earwax or spitting in someone's tea because they had annoyed them! You get the picture!

"Good God almighty, those two are a pair of utter bores!" he thought. *Self-righteous do-gooders who have such unutterably boring conversations!*

"Oh, I want to help the poor- oh I want to build schools for poor children or hospitals for the sick. Ooh, I want to

save the world!" Urgh! it was enough to make a person feel sick! It was all he could to not to fall asleep, listening to their dreary conversations!

"Five months I've wasted," he thought bitterly, *"five months and still, not a speck of dirt! What a bloody waste of time! "*

Septicus was very disappointed and almost despairing when a horrible, hideous, wicked thought entered his horrible, wicked head and slowly, creepily, his lips began to form themselves into a particularly nasty smirk.

"Hang on a minute!" he thought to himself , *" just because I haven't got any dirt on these two irritating goody shoes doesn't mean I can't make some up!" "WHY didn't I think of that before? Septic, you are a GENIUS!"* he thought triumphantly, smirking a horrible smirk-

and as he thought of all the horrible things he could do, his horrible smirk grew into a great big horrible smile.

Chapter Three - Enter Morgiana

Septicus and David were very close in age. In fact, Septicus was only six months younger than David and just as David was on the lookout for a wife, Septicus was looking for someone special to be in his life too.

Falling in love for Septic was hard though as he was already deeply in love with someone- himself! But being in love with himself could be a little lonely sometimes- I mean how many times can you blow yourself kisses in the mirror and tell yourself how wonderful you are? So Septic was looking for a partner in crime, someone like himself.

It wasn't long before he found her- the PERFECT woman or so Septicus thought. In fact, Morgiana was far from being the perfect woman, but she was perfect for Septicus because she was just like him! The only difference was that she was a girl. Like him, she only cared about winning. Like him, she wanted to rule over others and like him, she liked to make people tremble and bow to her will so, when these two met, they knew it was meant to be!

The minute they laid eyes on each other they knew. They KNEW they had found their other half, their partner in crime. When Septicus saw Morgiana across a crowded dance floor in the busiest nightclub in town, he could no longer hear the thumping pounding beat of the music for the thumping, pounding beat of his heart. *"My, that girl was eeevil!"* He loved the way she slid across the dance floor gracefully, like a cat. Her sharp violet eyes darted this way and that way around the room until at last, they fixed themselves on his. Her long shining black hair hung loose down to her waist and her tall, statuesque figure towered above all the other girls on the dance floor as she swayed to and fro to the music. *"My, she could be a supermodel!"* thought Septic, his eyes wide with excitement.

Morgiana too was admiring Septicus from afar. *Who was that blond Adonis on the dance floor with the broad shoulders and the icy blue eyes that could cut steel? Rrrrrr!* She had a feeling they were going to get to know each other very well. She loved the way he slithered across the dance floor like a snake. Morgiana wanted to know more.

Slowly, subtly, she edged her way towards him as she danced and she was glad to see that Septicus was doing the same. It would seem that the two of them had exactly the same idea! This pleased Morgiana and she flashed him a smile that gave him the courage to move closer and closer.

Morgiana was a beautiful girl and she knew it. Everywhere she went, heads would turn. Her long, thick, glossy, blue-black hair and her perfect, almond- shaped, violet eyes drew gasps wherever she went. Her tall, slim figure, her peaches and cream complexion, her perfect heart-shaped face, her beautiful blood red mouth with its perfectly shaped ivory teeth had earned her admiration everywhere she went for she truly was a beautiful girl.

You couldn't look at Morgiana just once when you saw that beautiful face. You had to look again and again and again, and people did look at Morgiana a lot which was why she knew she was special. She didn't need to ask her mirror who was the fairest of them all. One look into the eyes of ordinary lesser mortals told her all she needed to know. Everywhere she went, SHE was the belle of the ball!

Septicus, for his part, was feeling quite peculiar. For once in his life, Septicus was falling in love with someone other than himself and it hit him hard. He had to get closer to this girl and he made sure that he did! It wasn't long before Septic and Morgiana were dancing face to face, gazing into each other's adoring eyes. They didn't know how long they danced but it seemed like no time at all. They danced together perfectly.

Everyone around them- those lesser beings just faded away. Septicus and Morgiana only had eyes for each other. They made a perfect couple, and they knew it. Their good looks and their dancing drew lots of admiring glances from the people around them, and Septicus and Morgiana loved the attention. They knew that they were something special.

Well, that was the beginning of it. After the dance, Septicus told Morgiana everything about himself, the fact that he was a prince. He told Morgiana about his *"irritating bore of a cousin, David,"* and the injustice of David being the heir to the throne when he, Septicus Horrificus was taller and so much better looking! *"It's so unfair,"* he whined to a sympathetic Morgiana who seemed to truly understand him in a way that no one ever had before.

"So, let me get this straight," Morgiana said, *"You're TWO whole inches taller and better looking and STILL, he gets to be king! That's WRONG, you poor man!"*

"I know," wailed Septicus, burying his head in her lap as she comfortingly rubbed his back, *"It isn't fair!"*

"Well," decided Morgiana, *"We can't let this happen. We are going to have to do something about it and I know just the thing! Trust me Septicus, my darling, you are going to be king."*

"How can you be so sure?" asked Septicus hopefully, his heart beating wildly with excitement.

"I know because I am going to make sure of it." declared Morgiana with steely confidence in her voice.

"I know because I have ways of making things happen Septicus and now that you've told me about your secret desire to be king, I am going to tell you a secret about me. Do you want to hear it?"

Septicus, who was falling deeper and deeper for Morgiana by the minute nodded eagerly. He was all ears!

Chapter Four - Morgiana's Secret

Morgiana's secret was a terrible secret for Morgiana, beautiful though she was, was a witch and not just any kind of witch. She was a witch who practised the worst kind of malevolent magic that can harm people. She was a bad witch!

Witchcraft was Morgiana's weapon against the world. It had given her power. It had given her beauty and she was not about to give it up. She had used it to damage and destroy anyone who had come against her or angered her and now, in Septicus, she had found another reason to use it, this time to damage Prince David in the eyes of the world and to make Septicus king so that she, Morgiana, could become queen.

Since Morgiana had met Septicus that night she had begun to dream big dreams, bigger than she'd ever dreamt before! Not content with being a supermodel earning millions, now, she dreamt of becoming queen and like Septicus, she was willing to do anything to get what she wanted.

"So, tell me more about this David," she urged. *"He sounds like a dopey kind of guy. I need to know everything about him so that I can build up a picture in my mind.."*

"Well, the annoying thing is that everybody loves goody two-shoes David and they all want him to be king."

"OK, well the thing to do then is to make everybody hate him or better still, laugh at him," replied Morgiana, pondering deeply. *"Hmmm…. we need to damage him in the eyes of the public, ruin his popularity, make him look bad, ridiculous even and make you the most popular prince in Britain so that everyone will want to crown you king."*

"But the king and queen will never allow it," Septicus reminded Morgiana. *"David is their one and only son. I am just their nephew."*

"Then, the king and queen must be removed," said Morgiana callously, *"for us to reach our goals."*

Morgiana, for all her beauty, was a cold-blooded, ruthless person who was willing to ruthlessly knock out the competition whenever she wanted something badly enough. She saw life as being like a game of chess where she had to make all the right moves to win! Love, compassion, kindness, honesty, justice, being fair to others just didn't come into it for her. She didn't want to spend time thinking about what was right or wrong. She, Morgiana, didn't have time for it. All she wanted to do was to win.

"Hmm..OK… tomorrow is when we make our move," murmured Morgiana meditatively. *"Tomorrow, at midnight when the moon is full and high in the sky, I will do what needs to be done and soon, David and all his friends are going to get the shock of their lives Septicus my darling."*

"Oh my sweet angel, I can't wait," gushed Septicus, for truly, Morgiana was the most exciting woman he had ever

met- beautiful to look at and possibly the only person he had ever met who was more evil than himself. *"What more could a man want?"* *"Goddamit, I think I'm in love!"* he said to himself gleefully as he gazed into his mirror for the last time that night.

Chapter Five - Morgiana's Evil Plan

Morgiana was true to her word for the next night as the clock struck twelve, she sat cross-legged on the shiny marble floor of her home, surrounded by candles and brightly coloured crystals and stones. She drew a pentagram on the floor and placed David's picture in the middle of it as she began to chant in a strange language.

She closed her eyes and meditated carefully on each word she said with a blood-curdling ferocity and one by one, the candles began to flicker wildly. The moon shone high in the sky and in the distance an owl was crying "Tu whit too whoo" as if it knew some terrible tragedy was about to happen.

The wind blew in through the open window and lifted Morgiana's long raven tresses so that her hair danced around her as she chanted her eery spell from the thick, dusty old book she held tightly in her long slender hands.

It was the dead of night and the world seemed deadly silent except for the cry of the lone owl and the

quiet, meditative chant coming from Morgiana's blood-red lips.

Finally, after an hour of intense chanting, Morgiana relaxed and a triumphant smile slowly spread across her beautiful face as carefully, she blew out every flickering candle and went to bed.

"Tomorrow, everything changes," she murmured with a satisfied smile as slowly, serenely, she drifted off into a deep sleep.

The next morning, everything started as normal for David. He had an appointment at noon that day to open a new hospital in the centre of town and he had dutifully got himself ready for the occasion. He met his mother and father at the breakfast table downstairs with a cheery grin.

"Morning Mum and Dad!" he said cheerily, *"I'm off to the open the new hospital today. You never know, I might meet a beautiful princess there who's broken her leg!"*

"Don't be silly David," said his mother. *" I do wish you wouldn't make light of such a serious subject. I was married to your father by the time I was your age."*

"And look what happened there!" said his father jokily!

"Whatever do you mean?" gasped the queen horrified because, unlike David and his father, the queen didn't have much of a sense of humour. They knew this and they liked to tease her now again because she could be very funny without even meaning to be!

"Nothing... nothing... Phina. It doesn't hurt to have a bit of humour at the breakfast table sometimes. We're so used to talking about serious things."

"Well, being a king or a queen is a serious thing," said David's mother in an injured tone. *" I don't see what we have to be so cheery about when our only son is refusing to get married."*

David kissed his mother lightly on the forehead. *"You know I'm not refusing mother, I just haven't found the right girl yet. When I do, I will get married I promise. Until then, you'll just have to put up with me and wait a bit longer!"*

The queen sighed. She knew there was no use arguing with David. That boy always had a stubborn streak just like his father. There was no reasoning with him when he was like this. He would just make a joke out of everything. Sometimes, she really wished she'd had a girl. She felt outnumbered in this family of men.

It would have been nice to have had someone to go shopping with and have girly chats with and when David was a baby, she had so wished for a little sister for him but sadly, it had never happened.

Still, she had never quite stopped wishing and remembering those beautiful little pink dresses with the adorable little booties and bonnets she could have bought if she had ever had a little girl. Boys were so difficult to buy for.

Still, there was no point thinking about things that were never going to happen. It was all in the past now. Perhaps, when David got married and gave her grandchildren, she would have a little bonny granddaughter to dandle on her knee... when he got married... if he got married! She looked over at her only son and sighed. In spite of her exasperation, she felt a rush of affection for the boy. After all, he was such a good boy even if he was a bit silly sometimes.

She smiled warmly at David to his surprise, her earlier complaint forgotten. " *Make sure you wrap up warm David dear,*" she advised him. *"The weather man on the news said it was going to be very cold today, and don't wear that awful pin stripe suit you wore the last time you opened a hospital. It made you look like a banker, and remember, the press will be there so smile and don't talk too much or else they'll make up another silly story about you like they did the last time!"*

David smiled when his mother mentioned this as it reminded him of the last time when, following a joke he had made, the newspaper men had taken him seriously and had written in the papers that David was looking for a job as a janitor in the hospital.

David had meant it as a joke but newspaper writers were so desperate for shocking stories to sell papers that they had turned his joke into a serious article and for weeks afterwards, tourists had flocked to the hospital with their cameras expecting to see David, cleaning the corridors in a janitor's uniform!

Well, David knew better this time. He was going to be careful he thought as he finished his last piece of toast. You live and learn from your mistakes. This time, he would be a perfectly serious prince, no jokes and definitely, no

pinstripe suit! This time nothing was going to go wrong....
was it?

Chapter Six - David's Humiliation

The pressmen were like hungry hounds as they gathered round David in front of the hospital just as he was about to cut the ribbon and declare the new hospital open. They stood there, jostling each other, each of them trying to push their way to the front to get the best picture, each desperate for a better snapshot than the other to sell their morning papers!

"David! David! This way! Look at us! This way!" They shouted.

"Give us a smile. There's a good prince!"

David, being the polite prince that he was, turned and waved as he smiled. He knew that he had to keep the press happy or else he was likely to see another silly story about himself in the papers the next day because everyone knew that some of the press people could be spiteful and that they could make up silly stories about you if you upset them because many of them were desperate to sell papers.

And so, it was just another ordinary day as Prince David took up the scissors to cut the shiny, yellow silk

ribbon and to declare that the hospital was open for business.

Little could he have known what was about to happen. Everything was going so swimmingly well in spite of the constant click –click- click –flash- flash -flash of the pressmen's cameras until IT happened- the thing that was going to change his life forever!

Just as David had cut the ribbon and announced, *"I declare this hospital open!"* something happened that no one expected and instead of the usual cheer that went up when he opened a new hospital or school, there was a deadly silence.

Even the photographers stopped for a moment as their jaws dropped in horror before they quickly recovered themselves and started snap-snap snapping away at their cameras again, this time, faster than they had ever done before! They snap-snap -snapped away as if their very lives depended upon it! The camera men couldn't believe their eyes! They could not believe their luck! This was going to be huge! This was a SCANDAL- the biggest news story ever!

David realised from the horrified looks on people's faces that something was wrong and it wasn't just the looks of horror on their faces that did it either. It was the sudden chill around his legs, the sudden shock of icy cold wind biting into his legs which were slowly beginning to freeze in the cold December air. He looked down at his legs to see the reason why and realised with horror that his legs were completely bare and there, lying at his feet in an untidy heap were.... his pants!

"Oh my God!" he gasped silently to himself. *"Oh my good God!"*

Suddenly, for no good reason at all, it appeared that David's pants (trousers) had fallen down. All the press men were now furiously taking pictures of David, the future king of Britain, standing in the snow in...... his underpants!

David gasped and flushed a crimson red as desperately, he tried to pull his pants up! *"Oh my God, I will never be able to live this down,"* he muttered under his breath as he frantically, pulled his trousers up. *"I have got to get my pants back up before too many people notice!"* he thought but deep down, he knew it was too late! People had already noticed. As if to make the point, some people in the crowd looked away out of embarrassment.

Others tried bravely to keep their chins up and smiled politely as if they hadn't noticed but David could tell from the embarrassed looks in their eyes that they most definitely had!

Then horror of horrors, came the horrifying discovery that no matter how many times David pulled his pants up, they fell right back down again! He could not keep them up!

This was a dreadful situation. This was terrible. David was distraught. He knew he was in danger of becoming a laughing-stock. After all, how could a prince be a prince and a future king in his underpants with no trousers?

This... was a disaster!

David could hear mutterings of disapproval growing from among the formerly friendly crowd that now seemed to be turning against him!

"Outrageous behaviour!" said a grumpy looking man with a huge moustache and an oversized grey overcoat, *"not fitting at all for a prince to be standing around in his underpants like this in broad daylight!"*

"A prince with no pants!" sneered another, *"It's unheard of! What is the world coming to? It wasn't like that in MY day!"*

"You can't crown a man king in his underpants! It's not possible! It's not traditional," cried another. *"He'll have to be replaced if he doesn't want to wear pants!"*

And so, it went on and on and on. One by one, the crowd of people who had been so friendly to David now turned their backs on the poor innocent prince one after another.

And if that wasn't bad enough, there was worse to come! The next day the newspapers were covered in shocking headlines!

"Playful Prince Likes to Flash his Pants," screamed one headline!

"Prince David Wears Union Jack Knickers!" shouted another.

"Pantless Prince's Underwear Shame!" reported another.

"Say no to the prince who says no to pants!" announced another journalist in his article about the incident.

And so, it went on and on and on. It was horrendous.

Poor Prince David's life became an absolute misery. He couldn't go outside his door for the steely, disapproving looks of hostile people and cruel chants by cheeky roadside builders of *"Wot no pants? Wot no pants? Wot no ...Wot no... Wot no pants?"*

A particularly cruel pub owner called Harold renamed his pub, "Ye Olde Pantless Prince," and yet another called his simply, "The Pantless Prince." The news spread like wildfire and pretty soon, the whole of Europe was agog with the phenomenon of the Pantless Prince- as David soon became to be known!

Tears pricked David's sad ocean-blue eyes one afternoon as he heard the cruel chants outside his window for the hundredth time! How fickle people were, he thought sadly. How quickly they forgot all the good things he had done for them, the hospitals, the schools, the charity work. How quickly they forgot how much they had once said they loved him.

He had never known that people could be so cruel until now, until the terrible, sad day when he had lost his pants!

The king and queen for their part were terribly troubled by what was happening to their one and only son. They couldn't understand it at all. What had happened to the poor boy? Why couldn't he keep his trousers on? Why – oh- why did his pants keep falling down ? How had he developed this sudden mystifying pant allergy? Was it something he had eaten? Was it something that had happened to him in his childhood? What had gone wrong?

"Was it something we did wrong?" wailed the queen. *"How can he get married with no pants? I mean what self-respecting princess is going to want to tie herself to a prince who wears no pants?"*

The queen was right. It was really, quite embarrassing. All the princesses who had been keen to marry the eligible Prince David suddenly lost interest and found other princes to dance with. They might not be as kind and funny and charming as David was but at least, they wore trousers and they didn't parade around in their underpants!

Within a few short days, Prince David had gone from being a national hero to being a national zero, a laughing-stock, and the palace just didn't know what to do.

World renowned physicians (doctors to you and me) came in to examine him and to give their expert opinion. They all tried and tried but in the end, they all shook their heads sadly and after trying various special diets and potions to get to the root of the prince's strange "allergy" they left, shaking their heads, looking very grim indeed.

Counsellors came by the dozen, claiming that they could cure the prince by talking to him, by getting to the root of some childhood trauma that had re-surfaced in his adulthood and was causing his pants to fall down but after endless hours of endless talking about the prince's childhood and his school days, they all left with their heads bowed, broken by the challenge.

"Oh Nigel, what are we going to do?" cried Queen Seraphina. *"Our poor dear boy will never be able to go out in public again. He'll be doomed, doomed, I tell you! He can't be crowned king of the United Kingdom in his underpants! It's not traditional. It's not respectable. What girl is going to want him with no trousers? Who will have him now? We'll never have any grandchildren! Oh! What are we going to do?! What are we going to do?"* the queen sobbed on the king's shoulder.

To be quite honest, the king felt like crying too. He couldn't understand the whole damn business himself but he was a king and damn it, kings weren't supposed to cry like ordinary people. They were expected to be strong, stoical and majestic at all times and so, he bit his stiff upper lip and refused to cry.

Prince David saw the misery that his predicament was causing, and he felt terrible. He couldn't forget the cruel comments of the people who had once been his adoring public. Their cruel words went around and around in his head and stopped him from getting to sleep every night. Very soon, he began to look pale and drawn and took to wandering around the palace in his dressing gown.

When Amelia, his one true friend came to see him, she was shocked at how pale and tired he looked. *"Davey, I came as soon as I heard,"* she said. *"I'm so sorry. What's wrong? Have they found out why this is happening to you?"*

David shook his head miserably. *"No one can tell me why this is happening to me,"* he replied in a hopeless voice. *"No one knows."*

Amelia's eyes were full of pity for her prince who she secretly loved so well. She wished she could help.

"What can I do to help you Davey? Is there anything I can do?"

David smiled sadly at her efforts to help him and shook his head. Amelia, his one true friend, dear, loyal, dependable Amelia had been the only one who had bothered to come and see him since "the incident."

It hurt Amelia to see her friend looking so hurt, looking so unlike his usual self. She knew that something had to be done but what? What was the answer to this terrible situation? She knew she had always been able to make David laugh even when he was miserable but this was beyond her ken.

"You know, I can't think of any immediate solution apart from you wearing a kilt for the rest of your life!" she joked, hoping against hope that this might make him smile… just a little.

To Amelia's surprise, this did more than make David smile. At the mention of the word, "kilt" David's eyes lit up and a newfound hope started to make its way to his heart.

"Oh my God! Amelia! You've cracked it! You're a genius!" he cried. *"You've hit the nail right on the head! A*

kilt! That's it! That's the answer! That's just what I need! Why didn't I think of that? "

He grabbed hold of her hands and squeezed them, his eyes shining with excitement.

Amelia was taken aback by David's reaction. In fact, she was shocked. She had only been joking about the kilt but it seemed to have helped cheer David up so she wasn't about to complain.

"Don't you see Amelia? This is just what I need! I need to get away from here for a while until all of this dies down, until I can find an answer to this problem. Life has been getting unbearable around here for some time. It's been terrible but I can get away for a while and live in Scotland until I can find a way out of this problem and then, once I've cracked it, I can come back home!"

"But what about your parents," asked Amelia, *"What about me? We'll all miss you terribly!"*

"I know. I'll miss you too but if I stay here, I'll be miserable, and it won't any be good for any of us. I need to get away somewhere where I can wear a kilt without being noticed until I can find a way to get back into my pants again!"

And so, it was decided. Things were so desperate in England that David decided to go to Scotland in disguise as an anonymous Scotsman so that the press couldn't find him and so that he could have some precious peace at last!

The king and queen were a little less sanguine when David told them about his plans that evening.

"But David darling, where will you go?" What will you do?" sighed the queen, shaking her head sadly.

"Well, I can't believe it's come to this, my only son having to spend the rest of his life in a skirt!" grumbled the old king gloomily.

"Look on the bright side," said David, *"With a bit of luck, it mightn't be for the rest of my life. While I'm up there, I'm going to do everything I can to find a cure for my condition. Everyone knows that the Scottish people are some of the wisest people in the world. Maybe, I'll find some answers there. It's worth a try and at least I won't be a laughing-stock as I am here, walking around with my undies showing!"*

The queen knew better than to argue with David when he had got an idea into his head. He could be such a stubborn boy sometimes but as a mother, she knew it was her job to impart a few words of wisdom to her son before he went so far away. *"Well, make sure you get plenty of fresh fruit and vegetables when you go to Scotland David darling,"* she reminded him *"no junk food. You know it's not good for you, and remember to cross the road carefully and to wrap up warm. Scotland can be awfully cold this time of year, particularly for people who can't keep their trousers on!"*

David reassured his mother that he would do all of the above. He was used to having the same talk from his mother every time he went away! Really, it was quite embarrassing. He was twenty-five years old now, not a little boy but sadly, his mother never seemed to notice!

The king, knowing that David's heart was set on going to Scotland to find a cure, managed to pull a few strings and arrange for a place for David to live in the capital city of Scotland. He told the press that the prince was going away for a long vacation to the Honduras for some peace and quiet and to mourn the loss of his trousers and David set off not knowing that the biggest adventure of his life was yet to come!

Chapter Seven - Och aye the noo!

It was a cold, crisp December morning when Prince David stepped out of Edinburgh's main train station onto the concrete pavement and took a good look around. His mother had been right about the weather he thought as he felt the icy chill wind biting into his knees and blowing his thick, woollen kilt into a flutter all around him.

In spite of the thick, warm, woollen, knee-length socks he was wearing, his knees felt terribly cold. David shuddered as he waited for the taxi which was due to arrive anytime now to pick him up and take him to his new home. His father, the king, had arranged everything. *"Dear old dad,"* thought David. He could be a bit of a grump sometimes, but he was always there when David needed him. He had even arranged for David to wear an ingenious disguise to protect him from being mobbed or followed by the press when he reached Scotland!

Looking at the rather anonymous-looking man with the huge, heavy, red eyebrows, the thick mane of rich, russet hair and the big, bushy, red beard, no one

would have thought it was David, prince of the United Kingdom, standing there in the fetching black and green checked kilt which was now doing a merry dance around his slowly freezing knees.

In spite of the cold, David felt a huge thrill of anticipation as he stood there, waiting outside the station. For the first time, he was free just like any other ordinary person. No press, no cameras, no people staring curiously at him on the street or asking for his autograph. It felt good to be free.

The palace had even arranged for him to get a job at the bookshop in Edinburgh Castle because he had insisted on living like an ordinary person just to see what it felt like.

With his disguise, his home and his job sorted, David was ready and raring to go- to begin his new life. *"Life as an ordinary person,"* he thought, *"How exciting!"* David could not wait for his new life to begin.

Soon, the weeks passed by, and David got used to living in this new and exciting city. Everything was so new and so different. Majestic, snow- capped mountains towered above the city in the distance and contrasted beautifully with the busy town with its cobbled and paved streets, its imposing castle and the crowded shopping areas that were full of people on a Saturday.

In spite of a few early hitches, David had settled in well and was now enjoying his time working at the bookshop at Edinburgh Castle. The tourists all loved to see the red-headed, bushy-bearded man in the traditional dress of Scotland, standing behind the counter and many were the times when they took pictures of what they thought was a traditional Scotsman behind the counter. He became quite a fixture around the place.

The staff were also warming to David, this rather strange, kilt-obsessed person because he was a hit with the tourists and he seemed to have a very good heart, always willing to help out and pull his weight on the team.

Gone were the first awkward days when David had tried so desperately hard to be Scottish, saying things like *"Och aye the noo! I'm a gonna go up to the Highland Spring to do a Highland fling in ma kilt wi ma haggis!"*

He had realised from the rather strange stares he had been getting that perhaps, this was not quite the thing to say and do around these parts!

It was difficult for David because he hadn't known too many Scottish people before although he had studied the accent at the palace before coming to Scotland.

He was just guessing that this might be the kind of thing that Scottish people generally got up to in their spare time at the weekends but he soon began to realise, as the weeks went by, that Scottish people did not actually go up to the Highland Spring every weekend to do Highland flings in their kilts with their haggises so he began to tone it down a little after a while and people began to warm to him once they saw what a nice, kind, decent young man he really was in spite of his accent which seemed slightly off somehow and his obsession with wearing a kilt every day!

Among the staff at the bookshop, David met a particularly nice young man called Daniel Lindsay Stirling and the two soon became great friends.

Now, unbeknown to David, Daniel's grandfather was one of the secret wise men who live around the world in every country including Scotland, secret wise men who most ordinary men know nothing about.

These secret, wise men or sages had very special gifts that very few people knew about except for special people like Daniel so it was lucky that their paths crossed because Daniel's grandfather was going to become an important person in David's life and in finding the solution to getting David back into his trousers, but David didn't know that... just yet!

Chapter Eight - Morgiana Makes Mischief Again

While David was settling himself in Scotland, changes were happening in England, sinister changes. With David out of the way, Morgiana and Septicus now began plotting to get rid of the king and queen so that they could take over the throne and rule the land forever.

"Well, that's one down, two to go Septic my darling," said Morgiana *"until we are right where we belong- on the British throne!"*

"And the sooner, the better I say!" was Septicus's callous reply.

Morgiana was lazing on the black leather couch in the front room of her eighth-floor apartment which gave her panoramic views over the city. The city lights were shining brightly against the darkness of the night sky, which was dotted about with winking stars here and there, and she and Septicus were enjoying the view as they drank champagne in long, fluted glasses to celebrate their victory.

"I must say the headlines were hilarious – the Pantless Prince. Did you hear that's what they're calling him now! Everyone's laughing at him now the poor little princey, he's gone from hero to zero- I've never seen anything funnier" gloated Septicus, *"and it's all thanks to you my darling Morgiana. Oh my darling, I owe you so much. "*

"Yes, you do Septic baby, and don't you forget it or I'll tear your heart out and have it for breakfast!" replied Morgiana laughing.

"Angel, you have such a wicked sense of humour," whispered Septicus reverently, full of awe and wonder at this exhilarating, unpredictable woman who had changed his world forever and brought him one step closer to realising his dream. He couldn't stop looking at her and admiring her dazzling beauty.

Why, she was the only person he had ever met who was almost as good looking as he was! *"Everyone in the world must be so jealous of how good looking we are,"* he thought smugly as he took another sip of champers from his glass.

"Now for plan number two," Morgiana pressed on. *"We can't waste any time. We need to waste Mummy and Daddy. Get them out of the way so that we can move into the palace and get YOU the crown."*

"Go on," said Septicus with a wicked smile, "What do you suggest?"

"Well," said Morgiana, deep in thought, *"David was the king and queen's only child right?"*

"Right," affirmed Septicus. *"And?"*

"Well, think what it must do to them to have tragedy strike their only son. "I mean I'm thinking it could send them quite mad, don't you?"

"What are you planning Morgi?" asked Septicus, fascinated.

"Wait and see my love. Just you wait and see," replied Morgiana with a mysterious smile…

Chapter Nine - It's Enough To Send Anyone Round the Bend

The next morning when the maid went into the dining room to serve breakfast to the king and queen, she got a nasty shock for the king was behaving in a peculiar way.

"Hullo my dear," said the King with an unusually soppy grin on his usually sensible and serious face. *"How are you today?"*

"Fine thank you sir," replied the maid with a slight curtsy. *"What can I get you for your breakfast today, sir?"*

"Well, let's see, I'd like some penguin pate on rye bread with ostrich eggs and a nice, big slice of rhinoceros legs on toast...and.....and I'll...I'll have some pickled peas...pickled peas with speckles, pickled, speckled pretty pink peas please..!"

"Beg pardon sir but we don't have any penguin pate, pink peas or ostrich eggs and I'm not sure what you mean by rhinoceros legs on toast sir," the little maid replied with eyes like saucers, her voice quavering a little.

"WHAT?!!! What do you mean...you don't know what I mean- you insolent girl? Are you trying to be funny? I am the king and if I want penguin pate and pegs on toast...I will have some – do you hear?"

"Y-yes sir," mumbled the girl looking more and more terrified. She had decided it was useless to argue with the king at this minute, and a strange sense of terror began to build up inside her as if something unusual were about to happen.

She was proved right when suddenly, out of the blue, the king who was usually so dignified and majestic jumped on to the dining table and began to do a strange, sinuous belly dance before jumping off the table, doing the splits in mid-air and eventually, landing on his bottom on the floor! Then, standing on his head by the dining room door, he flapped his arms like a chicken, shouting *"Cock a doodle doo! A cow pooed in my shoe! Cock a doodle doo!"* over and over and over again!

The commotion he was causing woke the queen up and she came rushing down the stairs to see what was happening.

"Thank God," thought the little maid, relieved, *"Surely, her majesty, the queen will know what to do. At*

least, she's a sensible person, thank goodness," but the little maid's relief was short-lived because it became all too clear quite soon that all was not well with the queen either today.

The first sign of this was when the queen began rocking to and fro in her nightgown at the dinner table with her hair still in curlers, an avocado face mask on her cheeks and curlers in her hair. Then, she clambered onto the table (still in her nightie) and started trying desperately to swim across the table! *"Got to swim" she said breathlessly, "got to swim to the other side gel in case I drown! Hurry gel Hurry! Quick! Swim with me! Swim across the table before you drown in the tea!"*

The maid's eyes were as large as two very large saucers by this time and her hands were trembling so much that she was in danger of spilling all the tea in the teapot she was holding. She hurried away to the kitchen downstairs to tell more senior staff what she had just seen, and it wasn't long before they all came rushing upstairs to see just what was going on!

No one could believe their eyes to see their usually sensible and serious king and queen behaving in such a strange, inexplicable manner. What on earth had happened to them? What in heaven's name was going on?

It was heart-breaking to see the king and queen in this appalling state. Many loyal staff who had been with the king and queen for years had to look away to hide the tears welling up in their eyes at this sorry sight. What was happening to their beloved royal family?

First, the prince losing his pants and now, this? What on earth was going on?

In a panic, they decided to call for a doctor and for the king and queen's next of kin which was.... of course, the sinister Prince Septicus!

Now, this was just what Septicus had wanted all along– the moment that he and Morgiana had been waiting for - for so very long! With David out of the way, now, at last, Septicus knew his chance had come!

"Oh my poor dear uncle and aunt!" gushed Septicus to the press and members of the public who had gathered round the in his most sympathetic, honeyed tones. *"It really is terrible news. It seems that the king and queen were told that Prince David has disappeared in the Honduras; he is missing, presumed eaten by bears and the grief and the shock of it all has driven them both quite mad with grief. It really is very sad, but I can assure you that they will be very well taken care of in a private residential sanatorium until the end of their days. I will pay for their care from my own pocket because... I care!"*

"How sad," whispered a woman in the crowd.

"Absolutely tragic," said another.

"Well, it's not surprising," replied the first woman, *"considering what they've been through. It's enough to send anyone around the bend!"*

"Mmm... that's true. I'm just glad that Septicus is there to take care of them. At least, they can rely on him, not like that David. He went all funny all of a sudden. That Septicus is a lovely lad - just like his cousin David used to be before he went all funny and ditched his pants and disappeared Gord knows where!"

"Mmm..." the first woman nodded in agreement as she dabbed her eyes with her handkerchief. *"No prizes for guessing who our new king will be now,"* she sniffed and

then, blew her nose heartily into her already tear-dampened handkerchief.

She was right. There were no prizes for guessing who the new king would be – septic Septicus of course! It wasn't very long before the dear but now, completely dotty old king and queen were put away in a sanatorium and one Septicus Horrificus Germinicus and his new wife, Morgiana ascended the British throne to become Queen Morgiana and King Septicus Horrificus, the third.

Well-meaning people flooded the streets and flocked to the coronation to see this strikingly beautiful and statuesque couple being crowned king and queen of England and mingled with their tears of sadness for the old king and queen, were tears of joy for this exciting and beautiful new couple who were taking their place on England's throne, for surely, they made the most handsome king and queen in the whole world!

In fact, it was true to say that all the people around the world who saw the coronation taking place on their TV screens were impressed by what they saw of the glamorous couple but that was only because none of them could even begin to imagine the terrible, horrible things that lay ahead in the months to come…

Chapter Ten - Mayor Morris Meets the King

The first sign of trouble was when Septicus met the new mayor of London, Morris Ronson. Morris was a pleasant sort of chap although he did have a slight problem with static electricity which often made strands of his very fair hair stand on end on the top of his head, giving him that "just got out of bed" look.

Many... many... were the times when he coated his hair in strawberry-scented hair gel, trying desperately to get his hair to stay down after a journalist had asked him if he was advertising the bed head look but to no avail! It just didn't help at all! It was really quite embarrassing!

Right in the middle of a television interview- up his hair would pop, and he would look just as if he'd just stepped out of a wind tunnel all over again!

Still, the people of London forgave Mayor Morris his hair issues because he was a decent chap, honest, good hearted with an A plus sense of humour. He made people laugh and everyone likes someone who

can make them laugh and so Mayor Morris was a very popular man, well-loved and rightly so.

However, when Morris went to meet the new king for the first time one fateful morning, all that was about to change!

For a start, Septicus was not impressed by this blond headed "buffoon" as he saw it with the funny haircut. *I mean - was he really serious with that cockatoo hair! Had the man never heard of a styling salon? I mean- really! Some people could be so sloppy these days. Had they never heard of personal grooming at all? What was the world coming to?* The king groaned inwardly as he laid eyes on the mayor for the first time.

Mayor Morris, on the other hand, was thinking something different. He was marvelling at how magnificent the king looked, how majestic, how imposing. He was really quite impressive. He could tell they were going to be great friends....... or so he thought...... until Septicus opened his mouth!

"You may kiss my hand or.. ... my foot," said Septicus imperiously, *"I like to give people a choice.... because THAT is the kind of man I am!"*

"Of course, your m-majesty," replied the mayor, opting for the hand! He could tell at that moment that this was going to be an interesting meeting.

Well, he wasn't wrong. The meeting was interesting but not in the way that he had hoped. After only half an hour of being in the same room together with the new king, Morris left, red-faced, feeling a sudden, desperate need to get as far away from the new king as possible.

Septicus, for his part, had not been his usual charming self that morning. He and Morgiana had had a row about something trivial and silly, so silly that he couldn't even remember what it was any more, but it had put him in a bad mood and then, the sight of that dreadful cockatoo hair and that ruddy face had enraged him even more.

How DARE anyone come to the palace without spreading the appropriate amount of time on their personal grooming and their hair?!!! Honestly! It was an insult to him, the king! It was not good enough!

Poor Mayor Morris, for his part, was bewildered. Prince Septicus...or King Septicus as he was now had a reputation for being charming and kind, much like his poor, unfortunate cousin David. What on earth had got into him? He seemed so different, so changed from the kind and friendly prince they all used to hear about.

Everyone had had such high hopes for him on coronation day and now, this! What was going on?

Morris looked down mournfully at the piece of paper in his hand- a cheque from the king for a very important charitable cause, the mayor's own charitable fund for homeless people. It was well.....rather sad… disappointing even.

That was the heavy feeling in his heart he decided- disappointment. The meeting with the king had been disappointing- very disappointing.

And that was how it started – the feud between Mayor Morris and King Septicus. It wasn't long before things like this began to build up and the well-meaning and kindly

Mayor Morris began to get find himself on a fast -moving collision course with the new king!

First, there was the rumour that that irritating buffoon had spread about him that he was stingy! STINGY! Him! King Septicus who had very kindly and generously donated a whole POUND and FIFTY PENCE to the mayor's rotten charity for homeless hedgehogs or some other such nonsense!!!

"I mean- how dare he, a mere mealy-mouthed muffin of a mayor with messy hair criticise a great and good-looking king with excellent personal grooming skills like me?" thought Septicus petulantly. *"How DARE he? That moaning minnie of a mayor Morris had better watch his step, watch his mouth from now on or he'll be sorry,"* thought Septicus malevolently, *"very sorry indeed!"*

Well, it wasn't long before Morris annoyed the king again. Septicus was a gambling man and had decided to build a casino in the centre of town. Septicus loved gambling but he didn't want to build the casino to gamble in himself. He wanted to build it so that other people could gamble and so that he could get their money!

Being the cheat that he was, Septicus had a cunning plan to tamper with the gambling machines so that only a few people could ever win but lots of people could lose a lot of money- money that would go to him!

I mean it was such a bore, living on just £50 million a year he thought with a yawn. I mean seriously, how could people expect him, a great king, to get by on such a pittance?

It was awful to be a superior being, so much better than the lesser mortals around him, reduced to living in such horrible hardship! Obviously, something had to be done and obviously, a casino would be the answer!

Septicus was impressed by his own intelligence, and he tingled all over with excitement over his amazing idea until something or rather someone ruined his perfect plan!

Septicus found himself seething inside. That moralising, moaning muffin of a mayor Morris had stuck his oar in again and refused planning permission for the biggest 24-hour casino in the world which he, Septicus Horrificus, the king had wanted to build in the middle of England's capital city!

"I should have known it!" raged Septic. *"I should have known he'd make a mess of things! That moaning Minnie Morris is starting to get right up my nose! His attitude stinks! I am going to have him one day! He is going to push me too far one of these days! I just know he will!*

How dare he – how dare a pathetic nobody like him- defy ME? I am the KING!"

Well, the last straw for Septicus came very soon after that.

Just one month after Mayor Morris had refused Septicus planning permission for the gargantuan casino he had planned to build in the centre of London, Mayor Morris made his biggest "mistake," the mistake that was going to make his life an absolute misery for a long time to come!!!

Chapter Eleven - Mayor Morris Makes A "Mistake"

Now, in addition to opening new buildings, going to meetings, improving a city's public services like schools and hospitals, mayors help the police in their fight against crime, and Mayor Morris wanted to help.

Almost every other day, it seemed that there was some terrible crime in the news- criminals hold up bank and demand millions, gun crime on the rise, knife crime on the up. The headlines were endless. The people of London, brave though they were, lived in constant fear of crime because every other day, there appeared to be some new, horrible headline in the daily newspapers and on TV.

Mayor Morris had been working closely with the police to try and solve these problems in the inner city and had meetings with the local council, Londoners and the police to look at ways that neighbourhoods could be made safer for the people of London. He met lots of very brave policemen and women who did their very best to keep the people of the city safe even when it meant risking their own lives.

Mayor Morris was very impressed and rightly so, but a wise person knows that in any group or organisation, there is good and bad, and Mayor Morris was determined to root out the bad.

Now, Septicus had some friends in very high places who had some friends in very low places who they asked to do some very strange and suspicious things for them.

Some of Septicus's old school chums were now working in high-paying jobs as businessmen, bankers and others were working as senior civil servants, barristers and lawyers.

While most of the people in these professions were decent people, Septicus's friends were not! They say a man is known by the company he keeps and this was certainly true of Septicus Horrificus.

If anybody annoyed Septicus and his friends, crossed swords with them or upset them in any way, they could be ruthless. They didn't care what low trick they had to pull to destroy someone's life because they had no scruples whatsoever!

They would cheat, steal and tell any lie to hurt a person who had annoyed them, and it didn't take much to annoy them! All it took was a word or a look, a slight disagreement or a falling out and that person would be toast!

News readers read news reports almost every other day about criminal gangs in hooded tops from poor areas who roamed the streets of London, looking for trouble but what people didn't know was that they were not the only criminal gangs in London!

There were other types of criminal gangs who roamed the streets of London, rich criminals in sharp suits with good jobs who LOOKED respectable but who, when annoyed, could be just as deadly and just as dangerous as any gangster in a hooded top!

If they didn't like a person, all sorts of bad things would happen to that person and nobody would ever know why and who was really behind it.

These were men of money and they bribed, blackmailed and bullied people into ruining the lives of innocent people they didn't like. Some of these men even had contacts in the police!

While most of the police were decent, hardworking people, there were some among them who were in the pay of Septicus and his sinister friends, ready to cover up any evidence of the crimes committed by their secret pay masters.

It was all quite sinister and frightening for it was a deadly game that these shadowy characters played. They played with people's lives – the lives of every day, ordinary, innocent people with hopes and dreams and futures which could be callously ripped apart and destroyed by cruel criminals in sharp suits who hid behind their wealth and power, the appearance of respectability and the people they got to do their dirty work for them.

It was against this backdrop that Mayor Morris was about to make the biggest discovery of his life.

While looking into a police enquiry into a burglary that had taken place, he discovered that someone from the police had hidden evidence that would lead to the criminal being caught.

Morris could not understand why this would happen until on further investigation, he found that the policeman investigating the case had taken a very handsome bribe from a very "respectable" gentleman businessman named Damien Fox who just happened to be an old school and university chum of you've guessed it.... one Septicus Horrificus!

Morris was determined to uncover why this had happened and in time, it emerged that Damien had paid a gang to burgle the house of his business partner who was taking him to court for money laundering and fraud. He had paid the gang to trash the man's house and steal the evidence against him.

Then, he paid a corrupt policeman to "investigate" the crime and cover up the evidence against the criminals and him!

It was a long trail of dirt that led to some very shocking revelations and Damien, now exposed as a scoundrel, lost his job and his reputation and ended up in jail for the next fourteen years!

Well, Septicus was livid when his friend called him up in the middle of the night, crying for help! How dare that meddling, interfering busy-body of a mayor embarrass his old pal Foxy Fox? Who did he think he was- meddling in other people's affairs this way? *"This is just the last straw!"*

"That moaning Minnie Morris needs to be stopped in his tracks!" he announced to Morgiana that night. He has just made the biggest mistake of his life and he is going to PAY!

That meddling, moaning muffin of a mayor is going to learn the hardest lesson of his life and he is going to learn it...... FAST!"

Chapter Twelve - Loss of Pants- Causes and Cures

Meanwhile, in Scotland, Prince David, now settled in the capital city of Scotland, was doing all he could to research his condition. He did everything possible to find a cure. He went to the library and pored over the books in the health and beauty section but found nothing. He searched on the internet, typing, "Loss of pants, causes and cures," in the search engine but still, nothing! He typed in "Pantlessness, curable or incurable condition?" But all this he did to no avail. He could find absolutely NOTHING on the subject!

He found information on spontaneous combustion but there was nothing on spontaneous pant-fall!

Months had passed. Winter had turned to spring. Spring had turned to summer. Summer had turned to autumn and then, back to a blustery, biting cold winter again and still, he had no luck! He had spent almost a year of searching and had ended up with no information at all! He was losing heart fast and beginning to think that he would never find a cure-that he would be forced to live the rest of his life in a

skirt in Scotland which beautiful though it may be, was not really his home.

David longed desperately to get back to the old king and queen and to his best friend, Amelia. He had heard of the old king and queen's terrible predicament and had spent long hours on the phone, talking to Amelia about what had happened, asking her to keep an eye on his poor, unfortunate parents in his absence. Dear trustworthy Amelia, he knew he could rely on her if no one else but the one thing she couldn't help him with was the one thing that kept him from going home. He couldn't face all those people again in his underpants! He couldn't go back home until he'd found a way to get back into his trousers.

He couldn't forget their cruel words when he had stood there the previous winter shamefaced in the snow, freezing in his underpants! He knew he had to get his pants back on and his life back! But how? How was it going to happen? After a year of being away and finding no answers, he was beginning to lose hope that things would ever change.

The funny thing is that good things happen sometimes when we least expect it when all hope seems to have been lost!

David had taken to visiting his good friend Daniel Stirling at the weekends and spending time at his flat, watching the sports channel and talking about who scored which goal and how and where and when.

Over time, he and Daniel had become fast friends. They did almost everything together. They were like two peas in a pod. David had never had a brother and he and his cousin Septicus had never really been close, so meeting Daniel was a revelation to David.

For the first time in his life, David knew he had found a real friend, someone warm, sincere and real who liked him for himself, not just someone who wanted to be with him because he was a prince.

Daniel had no idea who David was. David took care never to take off his disguise until he was back at home alone in the safety of his own flat. David, for his part, admired Daniel for his warmth, his honesty, his generous spirit (he didn't mind sharing his time or his food with David) and his raucous sense of humour.

Daniel couldn't have asked for a better friend. There were times when he longed to tell Daniel the truth about himself but fear always held him back- the fear that he would be ridiculed - laughed at.

After the way that people had turned on him in England, he didn't know if he could trust anyone ever again apart from his parents and Amelia.

Still, Davey and Dan had some good times together, watching the sports channel, munching on snacks every Saturday and downing a few cans. Sometimes, Daniel's girlfriend Sarah would come around and watch the footie with them. Sarah was pretty cool David thought. She loved sports and she knew a lot about rugby and football unlike Amelia who didn't even know what an own goal was which was apparent once when they had watched a match on TV and Amelia had cheered when a player in David's favourite team scored an own goal!

When David pointed out that it was an own goal, she had replied "Well, of course it's his own goal silly! Who else's would it be? We just saw him score it!"

This comment and the countless number of times that Amelia had fallen asleep while watching a match and trying to look interested had made him realise that sports was never going to be one of her passions! She was more of an arts girl. She loved music, dance, art, literature. She knew very little about sports.

Now, here he was with a new best mate, someone who could understand the beauty of the game and who didn't fall asleep every time a match came on!

"Aah!" he sighed contentedly as he downed the last of his drink and sat back on the sofa. *"Thank God Mother's not here to see this he thought. She'd have me using a glass and eating from a plate!"* It was so good to be living the ordinary life with no pomp and no ceremony even if it was only for a while!

David had deliberately avoided talking to Daniel about anything serious or deep. Unlike his deep friendship with Amelia, his friendship with Dan had been based on just having fun and having laughs and being lads together but one night, that friendship turned into something a bit more serious.

It all began when they were slumped in front of the TV after watching hours of sports on TV and shouting at the TV screen. David turned to BBC1 to watch the news and there on prime-time TV was the scandal about Septicus's sinister friend, Damien Fox.

David could not believe what he was hearing. This kind of corruption was unheard of in England until now. What was going on? People in suits behaving like criminals? What was the world coming to?

"Terrible business that, all the stuff that happened with the royal family," said Daniel munching on his last piece of pie. *"You've got to feel sorry for those guys. One terrible tragedy after another.*

First, that David loses his pants and then, goes AWOL for months. Then, the king and queen go absolutely bonkers and end up in a looney bin and finally, you get this Septic guy on the throne, and he turns out to be a crook or closely connected to one!

How much worse can it get?"

"Yes, well, it was rather strange about what happened to David," said David cautiously, trying not to give too much away, *"No one could work out why he developed this sudden mysterious allergy to pants. There didn't appear to be any medical cause for it."*

"Well, of course not," replied Daniel taking a swig from his can. *"That's because it's got nothing to do with anything medical. It's obvious isn't it?"*

"Is it?" asked David in trepidation.

"Well, to the untrained eye and the unschooled mind, maybe not but to those who know, it is."

"What- what do you mean? What is it?" asked David who really didn't know.

"Witchcraft of course!" announced Daniel matter of factly, taking another swig from his can and belching shamelessly. Then, seeing David's shocked expression, he added

It's the occult, see? It's hidden. That's what occult means. It means hidden- hidden from the untrained eye, the unspiritual soul who knows nothing of metaphysics or the secrets of the universe and things unseen, etcetera etcetera."

"Huh?" was David's rather unimpressive response to this sudden revelation from his friend. He was well and truly knocked out over what Daniel had just said. This was a side to Daniel- a deeper, more thoughtful side he had never seen until this minute. Daniel was usually so down to earth and well, so un-extraordinary for deep thinking and talk like this!

"Look, I know it sounds far-fetched when you talk about it in the cold light of day but trust me my son, the occult exists," added Daniel, seeing the astonished look on David's face- *"not the kiddie fairy tale kind of witchcraft with flying broomsticks and magic wands and people turning people into frogs and toads. That's kid's stuff - pure fiction. That's not real. The real occult is completely*

different and it really exists. Just type in occult or witchcraft into the search engine on the internet and you'll see what I mean! That's the real stuff! I promise you!"

"How do you know all this?" asked David breathlessly. His eyes were shining now with real interest and he was all ears.

"Ah, well, that's easy. My grandfather is a sage, one of the few left in the world today, you know wise men who know things other people don't know! Most people don't even know that guys like my grandpa even exist any-more!"

David couldn't believe his ears. This was unbelievable-too good to be true. Down to earth Daniel- Daniel who seemed so normal and ordinary, talking like some holy transcendental sage! This was truly incredible. All these months, David had been searching for the key, the answer to his problem and here it was staring him in the face!

"So, if this is witchcraft, my trousers falling down, there must be a way to reverse it, right?" he asked tentatively, silently praying that the answer was *"Yes."* "Please God, let it be yes!"

Daniel sighed deeply and shook his head with all the gravity of a man weighed down with all the secrets of the universe. *"Aye,"* he replied at length, *"but it's not easy to reverse a spell. It takes patience and perseverance and only a good person with a clean heart and a good soul can reverse it - not everyone can make it happen."*

David decided at this point that he could hold back no longer. Now, was the time to come clean.

"Well, I need to make it happen," he announced with a note of such urgency in his voice that it took Daniel by surprise, *"and I need to make it happen fast Dan, my man. I need to meet your grandpops to ask for his advice. It's really important. I need you to help me. I'm in a bit of a fix."*

Daniel studied David's face as if seeing him for the first time. This was the first serious conversation that these two had had since they had met a year ago at the castle bookshop and they were just beginning to find out things about each other that they didn't know that underneath the jokey, laddish exterior, they both had hidden depths and thinking minds. It was quite a revelation for them both and from the look in David's eyes, Daniel could see that he was deadly serious.

"I'll do everything I can for you David," Daniel reassured him solemnly *"and that- my son- is a promise."*

Chapter Thirteen - Noodle in the Wind

Daniel needed to do something to help David and fast for when Amelia went to visit King Nigel and Queen Seraphina at the sanatorium for the incurably insane, she could see that things were bad- VERY bad.

The once majestic king and queen were now reduced to living in a state of near oblivion, sometimes staring endlessly into space for hours at a time and at other times, talking absolute nonsense and total gibberish to one another.

Amelia was astonished to hear the strange things they were saying to each other. She had never heard anything like it before and in all her years at the palace, she had never seen the king and queen behaving in this way. It broke her heart.

"My dear, my dear," said the queen to the king, pointing at the blank wall in front of them " Can you....can you see that hole in the wall there.... can you.... because.... I can't!"

The king guffawed and the queen tittered as he confirmed that he too couldn't see the hole in the wall which wasn't there!

"My love," riposted the king, "You know, one day I am going to fly away, far, far away across the galaxy and across the Milky Way to the planet Mini Mars and grow ice chocolate cream and pizza on trees. I am going to fly my

dear ....right across the moon like.... like....... a noodle.... in the wind!"

"Very good. Very good, my dear. I always knew you'd do something interesting someday. It's been very boring being married to you all these years. You really are very boring you know."

At this, the king's face suddenly crumpled, and he began to cry. He cried and cried and wailed like a baby.

"You're a mean lady." he wailed to the queen. *"I don't like you any more. I'm not your friend any more. I want my mummy!"* Then, he began rocking to and fro and sucking his thumb, tears pouring down his face.

Amelia felt terrible to see the once majestic king and queen reduced to this sorry and pitiful state. What happened to make them this way? What went wrong? Why had all this misery befallen the royal family all at once- it had been one major catastrophe after another. It just wasn't fair.

She knelt beside the old king who seemed so small and helpless now, so far removed from the imposing, majestic, powerful being he had once been and carefully, gently, she wiped away the tiny rivulet of dribble that was making its way down his chin.

"See how the mighty have fallen," sneered the beefy security guard with a cruel smirk on his face as she left at the end of her visit that day.

"I wouldn't gloat too much," said Amelia with sudden steel in her usually soft and gentle voice, *"It could happen to you too someday. It could happen to anyone."*

"Not me love," said the guard with an arrogant swagger, *" Things like that don't happen to people like us."*

"I wouldn't be so sure," replied Amelia as she prepared to leave until the next visit. *"Anything can happen to anyone at any time. No one knows what's going to happen in the future. No one can ever know anything... for sure."*

Chapter Fourteen - David Meets A Sage

Amelia was wrong. There were some people who did know the future or who knew of possible futures depending on the choices that men made. These people were the sages- the secret sages who lived in all parts of the world whose existence was hidden from ordinary men. It was one of these sages who lived in Scotland that David was on his way to meet.

Daniel, like a true friend, had been true to his word and he had arranged for David to meet his grandfather, Samuel.

David had expected a sage to look different somehow. He had expected someone like Merlin, the famous wizard of Arthurian legend, someone with a long, flowing white beard, flowing robes and a mystical glint in his eye. In fact, what he found was something quite different.

Daniel's grandfather looked just like any other grandfather. He had short, white hair with streaks of silvery grey, woolly slippers and normal clothes, a grey woolly jumper with grey woolly trousers and a

white cotton undershirt, nothing really out of the ordinary.

Unlike his long, tall, skinny, gangly grandson, Daniel's grandpa was smaller as if he had shrunk a bit over the years like a jumper that had been left in the washing machine too long but overall, he looked pretty ordinary just like anyone's granddad.

David must have looked surprised because Samuel said, *"You know son, the first lesson in life is that you mustn't judge a book by its cover. Things are not always what they seem to be on the outside. You have to look deep to find the truth about a person. You can't always judge by appearances."*

David knew that from his experience with the oh so handsome but vain Septicus so he didn't argue.

"So, what can I help you with my lad?" asked the old sage kindly with a warm and friendly twinkle in his eyes.

David told him all about his problem, the pants falling down and never staying up again, the king and queen's sudden onset of insanity. He told him everything in the strictest of confidence because true sages, he knew, always kept their word and their confidences.

After a year of holding everything in and smiling through his hidden tears for the disaster that had befallen his family, it was good to let it all out at last and have the benefit of a sympathetic ear!

The sage listened carefully to David as he poured out his heart. He sat there in his favourite armchair, nodding his head thoughtfully and looking grave.

"I've looked everywhere for answers," explained David *"and I was just about to give up until Daniel told me about you and about the transcendental..."*

Samuel sighed deeply and nodded wisely once again.

"Aye, it's true. It sounds to me like that's just what it is. All these calamities at once happening to innocent people who have done no harm to others has to be the work of an evil one. Too much has happened in your short life all at once to too many people for it ALL to be coincidence. This story reeks of the foul influence of malevolent witchcraft."

"But how is it that no one seemed to know this?"

"Because people are afraid of talking about it. Hundreds of years ago, people became hysterical to the point that anyone who had a grudge could call their enemy a witch and have them put to death. Hundreds of innocent people died because of it and ever since then, people are afraid to speak of it in case it brings back those crazy times again and besides, most people don't even believe in the unseen any more."

David was astonished by what he was hearing.

"So, what do you do if you think you're the victim of witchcraft? Say nothing? Do nothing?"

"You say nothing to people you don't trust," was the sage's wise reply.

"You don't accuse people of witchcraft because it's very hard to prove and no one wants to go back to the bad old

days of the witch trials again with innocent people being accused left, right and centre so you keep your counsel. However, there is something you can do to protect yourself and reverse the spell," he said, *"but you have to be a very special person to do it. You have to be worthy."*

By now, David's heart was beating very fast and his eyes were shining bright with the rekindled light of hope, hope which had been dying a slow, painful death over the past year after disappointment had followed disappointment for so long.

"Tell me, is there anyone who could gain by harming you and your family, by forcing you all off the throne at once?" asked the sage.

David sighed deeply. It wasn't hard to work out.

"My cousin Septicus," he replied. *"He's always resented me being the centre of attention even when we were boys. Now, that we're all out of the way, he gets to be the king and rule the nation."*

"Well, there you have it my son. Septicus is the key but you can't accuse him, not unless and until you can prove it and the most important thing for you is to, first, reverse the spell and get back into your trousers."

"But how can I do that?" asked David. *"How can I break the spell?"*

"Never fear my lad," was the sage's reassuring reply. *"Never fear. That's where I can help but you have to listen*

to all I tell you very carefully and you have to be patient and strong. Can you do that?"

David nodded his head eagerly, his eyes shining very brightly now with the fire of excitement and a newly recovered hope.

He was all ears!

Chapter Fifteen - Mayor Morris Gets to the Bottom of Things

While David was making headway in finding the secret cure in Scotland, Mayor Morris was having a very different experience in England because all of a sudden, he had found himself at the centre of a very strange and baffling controversy.

He noticed it soon after he had Damien Fox arrested for fraud and money laundering. Everywhere he went, people were looking at him oddly, whispering behind their hands and tittering behind his back. It was all very strange. Poor Morris couldn't understand it. What was on earth was going on?

All the people of London had adored him, the loveable mayor of London but now, all of a sudden, something had changed. Funny stares, odd looks, people hurrying hastily out of the room whenever he entered- had led him to conclude that all was not well. It was all rather baffling for the honest, down to earth, jolly man who had always got along like a house on fire with his London constituents... until now.

Mayor Morris complained about this to his wife, Laetitia Doris at breakfast one morning.

"You know Letty my love. I think there's something rather odd going on," he said thoughtfully chewing on a

piece of toast. *"I can't understand it. Everywhere I go, people seem to be avoiding me, giving me funny looks, walking away from me. It's all rather strange and I wonder... whatever can it mean?"*

Now, Laetitia Doris was a fine specimen of a woman, tall, well-built and robust with flame-coloured, Titian hair, fine green eyes and a strong determined chin. She was very protective of her husband Morris. He was such a dear sweet boy and it hurt her to see him looking so mournful and so sad.

"It's probably nothing my love," she reassured him. *"You're being too sensitive sweet pea. It's just that time of the month again. Now, hurry up and finish your toast. There's a good boy!"*

Mayor Morris knew better than to argue with his fiery wife Letty for she was a very determined, good-hearted woman who was always convinced she was right! It was easier to agree with her he thought just for the sake of peace and quiet and an easy life.

"All right my love," he said as he downed the last of his tea and donned his jacket. *"You're probably right. I'm just being a bit oversensitive no doubt. I'll see you later."*

He was making his way to the door as he said this and with a cheery *"Cheerio!"* he was gone, the door slamming shut behind him.

Laetitia Doris Ronson picked up the tea-stained cup her husband had left behind on the table with the plate that was covered in toast crumbs and sighed.

Why, oh, why did he always forget to wash up after himself? *She* always did the washing up right away! She hated to see crockery and cutlery festering in the sink for hours but loveable though her husband was, he never did seem to be able to wash up after himself right away.

It was a leftover habit of his student days when he and his flatmates had left piles of washing up in the sink for days, each hoping that the other would do it first until they were reduced to eating with plastic cutlery and paper plates!

"Here we go again, someone forgot to tidy up after themselves!" she thought grumpily to herself as she picked up the dishes, arranged them carefully in the dishwasher and switched it on.

After washing the dishes, switching the dishwasher off and rearranging the cups and plates neatly in the drying rack by the sink, she headed off to the post office to post a very important letter and to buy some stamps.

On arriving at the post office, Laetitia Doris found herself standing behind two very sweet-looking older ladies who were waiting in the queue to collect their weekly pension.

They may have looked sweet but what Letty didn't know was that these two ladies, Mavis and Ethel, were a pair of yabbering, jabbering gossips of the highest order. Cute and sweet little grannies though they were, the thing they loved the most in the world was gossip, juicy, shocking gasp-inducing gossip!

These two were the experts on all the gossip around town. They bought all the gossip magazines every week and oohed and aahed and tut tutted over the latest outlandish magazine stories. Woman becomes a man and then becomes a woman again- Man marries wife's sister's husband's labrador- famous popstar abducted by aliens and turned into shortbread biscuit... and so on and on and on!

These two cute little ladies were not so cute when they got down to some serious gossip as they had decided to do in the post office queue today.

It was lucky for Laetitia Doris that she ended up standing behind those two chattering ladies that day for she was about to find out some very important information that was going to change her husband's life forever!

"Ooh, did you hear the news Mavis?" crooned Ethel.

"What news Et?" enquired Mavis.

"The news about Mayor Morris. Ooh I used to think he was such a nice young man. Ooh, it seems I was very wrong- very wrong indeed."

"Whatever do you mean Ethel?" asked Mavis, her ears burning, eyes all agog.

"Well, my sister Maggie told me that her friend Beryl told her that her neighbour Gertie told her that her

hairdresser Betty told her that the man at Bingo's wife told him that she'd heard some dreadful news about our mayor from their postman!"

"Ooh whatever did he say Ethel?" asked Mavis, her eyes like saucers. *"Whatever did he say?"*

"Well, she said that he said that he's really an alien from outer space, not really one of us at all and that he's got a green bottom that glows in the dark and he's got pointy ears like Mr Spock and curly toes! They're saying that he's been sent by the Martians to Earth to take over the whole world! Ooh it just makes my toes curl Mavis, it really does!"

Mavis gasped and clutched her pension book and her bag with a trembling hand.

"Ooh! Well, I never!" she gasped *" .... he always looked like such a... nice boy! Whoever would have thought that he would have a green bottom that glowed in the dark! Ooh! I've never heard of anything like it in my life! Ooh it wasn't like that in MY day! Our mayors never even had bottoms! They were too polite! I don't know Ethel! What is the world coming to? Ooh. It doesn't bear thinking about! Oooh!"*

"Ooh, I know," tutted Ethel and shook her head, shuffling to the front of the queue, joined by a shocked Mavis who shook her head mournfully and tut tutted along in synch with her friend.

Well, the mayor's wife who had overheard all of this was astonished! Her poor Morris, being cruelly maligned, rumoured to have a green bottom that glowed in the dark, sent by aliens to take over the earth! She had never heard anything so ridiculous in her life! She made a note in her diary to phone a friend in public relations. Something had to be done about this rubbish that was being said about her poor, dear, innocent husband!

Meanwhile Mayor Morris was having another rough day at the office. People were still behaving very oddly around him. He would catch formerly friendly colleagues throwing furtive, hostile glances in his direction when they thought he wasn't looking and as soon as he looked up and caught their eye, they would quickly, abruptly look away. All very mysterious!

Others would openly look at him as if he was the worst person on earth and yet, others would hurry away whenever they saw him. It was most disturbing- bewildering even. Mayor Morris was at a loss. What on earth was going on?

Finally, unable to take it any longer, he made an announcement at the office meeting and spoke about his concerns, asking if something was wrong, if there was anything he needed to know about. He explained that people had seemed rather frosty of late and perhaps, just perhaps, something was troubling them. If so, could they please tell him so that they could talk it out and sort out any misunderstandings that may have taken place!

Well, if Mayor Morris had expected people to be honest with him, he was mistaken- sadly mistaken. People simply looked embarrassed, shuffled about a bit and then, said that nothing was wrong. They were all just stressed out because of the pressure of work but then, rather oddly, they all suddenly began talking repeatedly, obsessively about aliens with green bottoms that glowed in the dark and people with pointy ears and curly toes!

The mayor was stumped. What on earth was the matter with these people? Why were they behaving in a way that was so peculiar? Was it a case of moonstruck madness he wondered. It was all so very odd. What on earth was going on?

He soon found out- at the dinner table that night! Laetitia Doris, still reeling from her shocking experience at the post office earlier that morning, had decided to tell all to her husband. After all, he had a right to know, the poor boy! So, she told him everything she had heard at the post office that morning.

Suffice to say, Morris was not amused when he heard the news. His usually pleasant kindly face turned purple with rage and a strand of wispy blond hair shot up into standing position on the top of his head!

"Why Letty- It's a pyramid of piffle!" he cried.

"It's a tetrahedron of tripe!" he bellowed.

"It's a hexagon of hogwash!" he thundered.

"It's a dodecahedron of do do's doo doo droppings!" he roared, furious at this intrusion into his life and these

dreadful, appalling rumours and lies! It was awful. It was dreadful. It was not to be borne!

"Calm down Poppet, calm down now, there's a good boy," said his wife in her most soothing voice; she could see the poor man was really, dreadfully upset!

The mayor took a deep breath and counted to ten and when he had calmed down a little, he continued....

"But Letty my darling, Letty my love, why on earth would people be saying these cruel things? I don't understand."

Laetitia Doris sighed deeply and shook her ruddy russet curls.

"Who knows my love," she replied," *Perhaps, someone's jealous of you or you've upset someone and they're doing this out of spite. Whoever they are, they must be very very disturbed, and people need to know the truth. People must be told, and I know just what to do Poppet!"* announced the mayor's wife. *"I called my friend Sophie in public relations, and she suggested that we call a press conference tomorrow. She said we need to do it.... fast!"*

And so, it was – the next morning, a press conference was hastily called and Mayor Morris and his wife found themselves facing a barrage of questions and a myriad of flashing camera lights.

"So, Mayor Morris, is it true that you are an alien from outer space with a green bottom that glows in the dark?" asked one very edgy reporter, desperate for the limelight so

that he could make a name for himself as a hip and happening reporter about town.

"Most certainly not!" replied Morris. "If I had a green bottom that glowed in the dark, we would certainly have saved a packet on street lighting by now I can tell you!"

There was a guffawing in the hall following this riposte for even in the darkest of moments, Mayor Morris's humour shone through, and everybody laughed at this rather irreverent but funny remark.

"Mayor Morris, is it true that you have pointy ears and curly toes?" asked another reporter, a young, slender, female reporter in a grey suit with a slight nervous tic and round specs.

To gasps around the conference hall, Mayor Morris began peeling off his socks one by one.

"I'll show you whether or not that's true," replied the mayor. *"Here, you can see for yourself."*

He held up his right foot and then, his left and let the photographers take pictures of his toes which were very normal and definitely not curly! He then, turned his head to the side, pushed forward his ears and demonstrated to the whole crowd that his ears were definitely not pointy but shaped like everyone else's.

"Ok, Mayor Morris, so you've proved to us that you've got ordinary ears and toes but what about your bottom? Are

you going to show us your bottom sir?" shouted one particularly pushy journalist from the back of the hall.

"I am most certainly NOT going to show you my bottom sir!" riposted the Mayor, " for as you well know- it is not the done thing for mayors to be going around town, showing people their bottoms!"

The journalist, getting rather over- confident, continued further with his line of questioning,

"But how do we know that you haven't got a glowing green bottom unless we see it for ourselves Mr Mayor?"

"Well, you'll just have to take my word for it," said the mayor, now becoming rather red in the face. Despite his sense of humour and his smooth patter, he was beginning to feel rather uncomfortable now. It was really rather tiresome, not to mention embarrassing for a person- all this silly talk about bottoms!

"Well, have you got a witness who could vouch for your bottom sir?" the pesky journalist persisted.

The mayor by now was flushing a deep beetroot red. For once in his life, he was well and truly lost for words....

"Well, I-I...." he stuttered, "desperately trying to think of something witty to say.

Now, that was when it got all too much for Laetitia Doris, seeing her poor dear Morris struggling like this after being thrown to the wolves! She knew she had to butt in and help the poor boy for he was dying out there.

"I am a witness!" she announced.

"I... have seen the mayor's bottom!"

There was a sudden hush in the room. It was so still you could have heard a feather drop! All eyes turned on Laetitia Doris.

"I have seen the Mayor's bottom," she announced bravely *"and I can promise you, it is definitely not green! It is as pink... as his face!"*

There was a titter across the room and a few laughs were hastily disguised as coughs by some very amused reporters who were loving every minute of this rather interesting and unusual press conference.

"So, are you saying Mrs Mayor," smirked the journalist who was beginning to enjoy this banter a little too much for Laetitia's comfort, *"Are you saying that... your husband has a face like a bottom?"*

A horrified gasp rippled rapidly across the room at the impertinence of the overly bold journalist who seemed to be enjoying himself just a little too much and heads turned quickly from the journalist back to the mayor's wife to witness the response to this daring question.

"Most Certainly NOT!" cried Laetitia Doris, outraged at this slur on her husband's good name! *"My husband does not have a face like a bottom! He has a perfectly nice face! A good, kind, honest, sweet face,"* she added, her voice breaking a little with the emotion of it all.

"Mrs Ronson. You have made a shocking revelation here today that you have seen the mayor's bottom," said the female journalist in the grey suit, brushing back a strand of mousey brown hair that had come loose from her pony-tail which swung from side to side as she interrogated the mayor's wife.

"How exactly did this happen? I mean- after all, everybody knows that most grown-ups are far too sensible to be even thinking about silly things like bottoms, let alone looking at them!" she added with a sly smile.

The mayor's wife looked horrified, mortified and embarrassed all at the same time! She blushed a deep rich rosy red, a blush that ran to the very roots of her Titian tresses.

"W-w-well," she stammered, *"It was... it was qu...quite by accident of course! I mean when you live with someone, these things can happen....accidents I mean. I-I-I saw the mayor's bottom quite by accident and I only saw a tiny, tiny little bit of it but I am certain... I am quite certain.... that it definitely was not green. It was very definitely a very ordinary looking bottom....as bottoms go, not that I've seen a lot of bottoms of course,"* she added awkwardly, hoping that this would be the end of this dreadful barrage of nightmarish questions.

"Well, I suppose, we shall have to believe you, Mrs Mayor," sighed the first journalist with a slightly wry and cheeky look in his eye. *"We have seen the evidence- well, partly – I mean the mayor's ears and toes seem quite normal*

and his bottom, well, we'll just have to take your word for it Mrs Ronson." He pulled a pen from behind his right ear and began scribbling away furiously in his note-book.

"Any-Any further questions?" asked the mayor, praying silently, desperately, that the answer would be *"No."* Well, someone very high up must have heard his prayer because the journalists all seemed satisfied with their responses and chorused *"no"* together as they shook their heads and then, proceeded to pack away their notebooks and cameras, ready to disperse for the day.

"Whew!" The mayor and his wife breathed a huge sigh of relief that night as together they lounged on the large, cosy cream cotton sofa in their front room and had a celebratory cup of cocoa before trundling off to bed.

"Thank God that's all over," yawned the mayor sleepily as he shuffled towards the bedroom with his wife following close behind him after a long, hard, exhausting day.

"Yes, thank God that's all over," echoed his exhausted wife as she hit the pillows and drifted swiftly off to sleep, feeling safe in the knowledge that this ridiculous alien fiasco was well and truly over.

Or at least, that was what they thought..........at the time!

Chapter Sixteen - Morgiana Makes Mischief....Again!

If the mayor and his wife had thought they were safe now, they were wrong for the evil Morgiana and Septicus hadn't finished with them yet, not by a long chalk!

After the press conference in which the mayor and his wife had been mercilessly grilled by the press, the rumours had gradually been dispelled as word got around that the mayor wasn't actually an alien from outer space sent to earth to destroy the planet and that he didn't really have a glowing green bottom and funny toes after all!

Someone very malicious and very spiteful must have started those lies. Once the people of London realised this, the panic was over. People relaxed, life resumed, and everything began to get back to normal again.

But this was not good enough for Septicus and Morgiana. Septicus, in particular, was livid, roaring with rage that this irritating busybody of a mayor had

thwarted him and was still at large, back in the hearts of the people of London again!

"That damned fool! Why- oh - why did he have to show his flaming toes to the world to ruin my perfect plan? And how in hell and damnation did that bumbling idiot find out what was being said about him? It had all been done behind

his back as sneaky as you please so that he would never be able to defend himself, so that he would never be able to clear his name!

Someone very stupid... must have spilt the beans... someone with a big mouth must have opened their big, silly trap and told him everything.... but who? Who could it be? Dammit!" Septicus was driving himself mad, pacing up and down the palace, fuming at the dreadful injustice of it all!

"Never mind, Septic darling," Morgiana drawled, lounging lazily on the front room couch, playing with a strand of her beautifully coiffeured ebony hair and pouting in the mirror that she held in her perfectly manicured slender right hand. *"The game's not over until the cards have all been played as they say my darling and we haven't finished with him.... yet!"*

"Have we not, my love?" asked Septicus, a small glimmer of hope beginning to infuse his stone-cold, icy heart. *"What exactly are we going to do?"*

"What am I going to do - you mean, darling?" replied Morgiana smugly, a sneaky smile smouldering snakishly on her beautiful, blood-red lips.

"What are you going to do my love?" enquired Septicus fascinated by this exhilarating woman whose heart was just as cold blooded and hollow as his own. She had never let him down yet. God! He adored her!

"I am going to make the mayor look like a fool, a cold, calculating, lying fool!" said Morgiana sitting up suddenly as if possessed of a brilliant and new idea.

"And how are you going to do that my beautiful, witchy one?" asked Septicus, his heart pounding, hands trembling with the excitement of it all as fresh hope rushed like a tidal wave into his hard and hollow, stone-cold heart.

Morgiana tapped the tip of Septicus's nose playfully with a perfectly manicured fingertip.

"Just you wait and see my love. Just you wait and see," was Morgiana's mysterious reply.

Chapter Seventeen - More Misery for Mayor Morris

The day had started normally for Mayor Morris and his wife Laetitia Doris... well, as normal as it could be after that dreadful fiasco surrounding his non-existent glowing green posterior and supposedly curly toes! What a dreadful strain it had all been. Who could have been so spiteful and so churlish as to spread such wicked lies? There were some very sick people out there the mayor had decided. They just didn't know how to behave!

To get away from it all, the mayor and his wife had decided to go down to Brighton Beach for the next couple of days. The whole of England had been rocked by the recent scandal which had hogged the headlines and word had spread like wildfire about the mayor's supposed alien credentials but now, thank God and thanks to the healing power of public relations, the truth was out, and the row was finally over.

People all over London knew that they could trust the mayor again for he was truly an honest and good-hearted man, and everyone felt terrible about the

awful way they had treated their poor, kindly, honest mayor on a horrible lie!

The mayor, for his part, felt relieved that the truth was out and that things could go back to normal again but the strain of it all had drained him and he and Letty needed desperately to get away from it all....at least, for a while so, he had booked a couple of days of annual leave and was on his way with the lovely Letty by his side to the Brighton hotel where they had booked a luxury suite for a long weekend away from it all. *"Only the best for my Lettykins,"* he thought as he smiled lovingly at her while positioning himself behind the steering wheel of his car, ready for the long drive down to Brighton.

Letty, for her part, was looking forward to the long weekend that her darling husband Morris had booked for them- as a holiday was something they had both needed for a long time, but they had never seemed to manage it before because of the hardworking mayor's busy schedule.

"At last," she thought happily, *"At last, we're going to have a break from all the stress and strain of work and have a few days together just to ourselves."* She leaned back in her seat and closed her eyes. She was going to enjoy this she thought with a satisfied smile.

Unfortunately, as we all know, the best-laid plans have a way of going awry at the best of times and poor Letty had no idea what fate had in store for them that weekend or she might not have felt so relieved. She certainly wouldn't have smiled so much if she had known what was to befall them on that fateful weekend.

Well, it all began the next day. Mayor Morris and his wife had settled comfortably into their suite the night before and were now having a lovely day eating fish and chips and lazing on sun loungers on the beach by the seaside.

It was a good time of year for it was the middle of June, exactly a year and a half since Prince David had fled pant-less into Scottish exile.

The sun was shining in the sky. The sky was a beautiful, pale, powder blue with wispy, white cotton clouds dotted about, and the sea was an undulating turquoise mass of liquid heaven.

People covered in sun cream lotion were lazing about on the beach in stripey deck chairs. Others were splashing about ankle-deep in the clear, crystal blue water. Teenagers lounged lazily together on brightly coloured beach towels and screeched hysterically at juvenile jokes or pored over thrilling teen magazines to find out what had become of the latest heart-throb or teen sensation.

Everyone was in a summery mood, in sunny summer beach heaven. Everything was right with the world. Nothing could go wrong until, of course… it did!

The mayor remembered exactly when it all went wrong. He couldn't forget it. It was so awful. The first sign of trouble was the horrible shriek someone let out as he made his way down to the water to have a splash in the sea.

At first, the mayor thought that it was some teenagers larking about, screaming ear splitting screams as they were wont to do because of all the teenage hormones rolling around in their over-excitable, adolescent brains but unfortunately, he was wrong. The scream was not coming from a teenager at all but a middle-aged lady in a sun lounger who had just spotted a sinister, eery green glow, emanating from the mayor's sensible grey and white swimming trunks.

"Oh my Goodness! Aaah Aaaaargh!" she screamed, pointing frantically at the mayor's pants *"Aaaaaargh!"*

Everybody turned to see what the commotion was all about, and it was at that moment that all hell broke loose!

"Quick! Run for your life! The mayor's an alien!" shouted a large, heavyset man as he waddled away from the seaside.

"Oh my God, it's true! It's true! The mayor IS an alien!" screamed another woman, trembling to her very toes and running for cover behind an old beach hut!"

"He lied to us! He's been lying, all along!" warbled yet another woman as she hid, shaking behind her deck chair, making a slow but steady retreat away from the water's edge, taking the chair along with her in case she needed to hit the alien mayor with it at any point if his unpredictable alien ways got the better of him!"

Letty was awoken from the gentle snooze she was having on her deckchair by the commotion of it all and stared wide-eyed with disbelief at the very undeniable, fluorescent green glow that was emanating eerily from her husband's sensible grey and white swimming trunks.

What was the meaning of this? She knew her husband was not an alien! What on earth was going on? How could this be happening? It was all too odd for words. *"Heaven, help us all!"* she thought in horror as she noticed that the green glow was now spreading from his trunks up to his back and then, up to his neck and shoulders as if some alien force was taking over the man that she loved.

While the people on the beach ran screaming for their lives in a mad, manic rush, she ran towards the poor bewildered Morris gesturing wildly, shouting, *"Morris! There's a green glow coming from your pants! Your pants Morris! Your pants!"*

Morris, on hearing his wife's words of warning turned round to get a look at his posterior, desperate to see for himself this eery transformation that was taking place. He turned around again and again...... and....... again, but no matter how many times he turned around, his bottom... remained behind him! He just could not get a look at the damn thing!

Furious, exasperated, exhausted by the strain of it all, he began to do the unthinkable for a sensible mayor. He began to swear! *"Damn, bother, double damn and blast!"* he muttered furiously under his breath. *"What kind of a mixed up, crazy world is it when a fellow can't get a look at his own bottom to check it isn't going green?! It's not on! It is just NOT on! There ought to be a law against this sort of thing!"*

Not being able to get a look at his own backside was not the mayor's only problem now because soon, it became apparent that he had other pressing problems that needed dealing with… fast!

As the eery green glow began to spread steadily to other parts of his body, a crowd had begun to gather at the other end of the beach, a very angry, irritable, crowd which now started throwing bits of rock at the mayor and his wife.

"Get the alien! Quick! Call the police!"

"We'll have no green people here!" they cried as they lugged sticks of Brighton rock at the terrified mayor and his wife.

"Quick Letty, get in the car, there's a good girl!" shouted Morris to his fiery wife who was furiously throwing sticks of rock back at the crowd for she was determined give as good as she got.

"Stop that Letty darling and get in the car now! You mustn't go down to their level. You are the mayor's wife. It just won't do! Quick! Make a run for it NOW!"

He ran towards his wife, grabbed her firmly by the wrist and steered her towards the car which they had parked a few metres away from the beach front.

Hurriedly, they jumped in and leaving all their luggage in the hotel, they drove away with the mayor dripping water all over the seat as he drove towards London in his swimming trunks.

The next day, the papers were full of headlines about Mayor Morris and his great escape. It appeared- said the papers- that Mayor Morris and his wife had fled their London home in disgrace after it was revealed that he had been an alien after all and that the good, honest mayor of London had been lying to the people all along!

"Shocking!" said Septicus the next morning at breakfast as he read the papers with a smirk on his face while taking a sip from his cup of steaming hot coffee. *"Absolutely shocking! The scoundrel should be hung!"*

Morgiana looked at Septicus triumphantly and as their eyes met, they both burst into peals of laughter!

"I wish I could have seen his face!" cried Morgiana, her face pink with amusement.

"If only I could have been there to see that sanctimonious, sickening saint of a mayor get his come-uppance at last!" added Septicus with a ferocity that could have made fresh milk curdle.

"Oh, my mesmerising Morgiana, my own exciting witchy one, what would I ever do without you?" drawled Septicus pulling Morgiana onto his lap and planting a grateful kiss on her blood red lips. *"You've done it again my angel of the night. I knew that I could count on you."*

Morgiana ruffled Septicus's well-gelled hair ever so slightly with her silver and scarlet, manicured talons.

"You know you can always count on me, Septicus baby," she purred as she looked deeply into his icy blue eyes ....and smiled........ a chilling smile.

Chapter Eighteen - The Garden

While the mayor was languishing in hiding, David was having troubles of his own. David had made great friends with Daniel. They'd become best friends but despite his friendship with Daniel, something was missing in David's life, and he had begun to realise that the curious, nagging empty ache that was gnawing away at his heart was for his childhood friend, Amelia.

David was missing her terribly, her wit, her kindness, her soothing voice...her reliability, her good sense, her smile. It made his heart ache just thinking about her. He had never missed anyone so much in all his life.

He missed his poor old mum and dad too, even lay awake at night sometimes thinking about them, how to help them and get them out of the fix that they were in, but Amelia was weighing heavily on his mind. It was a heavy, heavy burden that David was bearing. Yet, still, bravely, patiently, he kept calm and carried on.

The world outside would have never known that this cheerful, helpful, courteous young man had a care in the world. It was that stiff upper lip that the old king had taught him to develop even as a child that got him through, that and dreams of the day when he would return home to England in triumph as the true heir to the British throne. He couldn't wait! But he knew that he had to take his time, be patient and prepare properly for the long and arduous task that lay before him before he and his people could finally be free. It was to this end that he spent months and months talking to Daniel's wise old grandfather Samuel.

He was learning about the dangers and pitfalls and demands of the arduous and difficult journey that lay ahead of him to break Morgiana's spell and to rescue his people from the rule of the newly-crowned tyrannous pair. David was preparing for the arduous, strenuous, pitiless climb up formidable Soul Mountain.

David was not one for mountain climbing generally and he certainly would never normally contemplate climbing a mountain alone because he knew it could be very dangerous, but Soul Mountain was different. Soul Mountain was a special mountain. It was not like other mountains but.... it wasn't going to be easy.

David had been warned by Samuel that he would face all kinds of tests and trials but that he could not afford to fail. He would have to push on to the very top of the mountain to win the coveted prize from the highest of high, invisible to the eye, the incomparable, indescribable one, the one who gave the sages their power and their gifts ...... of foresight and insight. He would have to patiently make the long and arduous journey to the top of the mountain to attain the prize that could set him and his people free.

David learned from Samuel that this gift of wisdom was more precious than gold and would give him the knowledge that he needed to set his family and his people free from the bondage into which Septicus and his evil witch queen Morgiana had thrown them.

It wasn't going to be easy, but David was the true heir to the throne and although this task lay heavy upon his young shoulders, he was determined not to fail.

In his earnest efforts to save the world though, it had never occurred to David that someone might need saving- someone very precious to him .... until one night he had a haunting dream.

David had had a restless night. It had taken him a while to drift off to sleep. Perhaps, it was the sound of the hail, pelting pitter patter against the window again and again and yet, again and the occasion rumbles of thunder and flashes of lightning that lit up the sky or perhaps, it was the cup of coffee that he'd had two hours before going to bed but it took him ages to finally get to sleep that night and when he finally did, he drifted off into a restless, peaceless sleep, punctuated by terrible, fearful dreams.

There she stood in front of him- his Amelia. He smiled in his sleep as he saw her from the back but when she turned around, his smile froze because of the look on her usually tranquil face. Her usually gentle, warm hazel eyes had lost their softness and had been replaced by a haunted look as if she were afraid, very afraid.

David woke up with a start. His heart was pounding fast. It was just a dream, so why should it affect him so badly?

He had been so busy with Samuel, preparing for the climb that he had not phoned Amelia for fourteen days. He had meant to phone her everyday but somehow, exhausted from working at the shop by day, doing simulated mountain climbing sessions at the local sports centre in the evenings, doing the odd weekend rock and mountain climbing courses and having preparatory lessons with Samuel at the weekends, his good intentions had fallen by the wayside even though he had been missing her terribly.

He decided to phone her the very next day before he lay back down to sleep. He needed to get at least a couple more hours of sleep as he was due in at work the next day and he couldn't function unless he had had at least eight hours of sleep.

After a while of lying there bored in the dark, he finally began to drift off for a second time. This time, he had another dream just as disturbing as the first.

As he drifted off to sleep, he began to see a garden, a beautiful garden full of bright and beautiful flowers in bloom. As stepped into it, he caught the scent of jasmine and roses. He breathed it in. In front of him was a sea of colours. There were rows of purple violets, followed by pink and white peonies followed by rows of violet roses and then, more rows of fragrant cream-coloured roses.

After the roses, there was a row of delicate, yellow daffodils, bowing their heads to the beaming sun followed by ruby red poppies which danced gracefully in the soft breathy fragrant spring breeze. It was a tremendous sight, and the natural fragrances in the garden were better than all the bottled perfumes in the world.

David stood there for a time and breathed it in, his eyes closed, breathing in the flowers in long, deep, luxurious breaths until something began to change.

When he opened his eyes, he found that something was happening in the garden...something strange. He watched in slowly mounting horror as the change unfolded before his very eyes.

First, something began to emerge from the garden's soft, moist, fertile soil. Tiny green weeds began to make their way determinedly through the surface of the soil.

As they grew upwards, they grew bigger and bigger, stronger and stronger until the tiny weeds had grown into huge monstrosities which were steadily and stealthily taking over the entire garden. It looked as if they were on a military march, their purpose fixed, deadly, unstoppable, taking over entire flower beds.

The flowers and plants that had grown so fragrantly and abundantly until now were being slowly but surely squeezed out, pushed down or choked to death by the new, menacing, sinister plants that were taking possession of the garden and mercilessly squeezing the life out of the flora that had flourished so beautifully side by side until now.

In place of orderly rows of beautiful flowers, each with its equal space, frightful, fiendish, menacing, monstrous weeds now multiplied and extended themselves greedily, haphazardly, graspingly across the soil, trampling down and choking the plants that had blossomed so beautifully and harmoniously before their merciless invasion.

This process continued until the garden that had bloomed so beautifully and fragrantly just a short while ago was overgrown with ravaging weeds which reeked to high heaven while all the flowers were lying on the ground beneath them- dead!

In just a few short minutes, David had watched in horror as the garden which had been a heaven transformed itself into a menacing, fearsome, horrifying hell!

David shot up in his bed, his heart pounding, palms sweating, as the dream vision faded as quickly as it had come. This dream was not like any other dreams he had ever had before. The sheer vividness of this dream made it seem significant, somehow real. He couldn't understand why he had been so deeply shaken by a mere dream.

David looked at the time on the clock on the bedside table and groaned. It was almost time to get up for work! He still felt tired after the stresses of the past week, and he did not feel refreshed or rested after his restless night of devastating nightmares and dreadful dreams.

Yet, as he had his porridge for breakfast and got dressed for work that morning, David knew exactly what he needed to do.

Chapter Nineteen - The Sage Speaks Again

So, you say that garden that was blossoming so beautifully just a few moments ago transformed itself into a bed of weeds?" Samuel asked David later that evening as David sat by the fireside in an armchair facing Samuel in his cosy little front room.

"Yes," replied David, "it was the strangest thing."

"And you saw your wee friend cryin her heart out like it was breakin?" he clarified.

Again, David affirmed that this was true. "But the strangest thing is that when I phoned her this afternoon, she said she was fine. She didn't mention anything about things being wrong. I guess it was just a silly dream after all. I have no idea why it affected me so much."

"Hmmm…….maybe, she is fine and maybe she's not," Samuel said cryptically. When David looked at him quizzically, he went on, "A dream is just a dream most of the time. Most dreams have no significance at all. I say MOST dreams but now and again, mebbe, ten percent of the time, they can be a source of inspiration or they can tell us things."

David sighed deeply and stared into the fire-place in Samuel's living room as if hypnotised by its orange and yellow flames.

"There was something different about those dreams though. They keep coming back, repeating again and again," he mused, thoughtfully. *"I just feel as if I ought to be doing something. Why do I keep having the same dream over and over and over again?"*

Samuel thought for a minute. David watched him thinking, his brow furrowed, his finger placed thoughtfully on his bearded chin. This time it was Samuel's turn to sigh.

"This girl of yours Amelia, does she talk about her feelings a lot or is she one of them that holds her feelings in?"

"Well, she does talk about her feelings with me but come to think of it, I've never seen her looking sad in all the years that I've known her. I've never seen her cry, not even when her grandfather died although I know she loved him with all her heart although.......come to think of it....she did seem to have a kind of puffy look about her eyes at the time."

"Well, there ye are then," said Samuel. *"She's a strong un. She's a brave wee lass. She doesn't let her feelings show. She's one of them that holds it all in. Just because she sounded right on the phone doesn't mean that she really is all right. She could be putting on a brave face. She knows you have yer own troubles son. You need to find out if she's really all right."*

"Come to think of it," pondered David, *"she sounded a little less chirpy than she normally does. Although her WORDS reassured me that everything was all right, I could*

tell there was something different about her tone. She wasn't her usual, lively, chatty self. You know, I think you might be right Sam. I've been a fool. She'd never tell me even if something was wrong. She'd be too worried about worrying me! Oh God! I've let her down!"

"There now lad, don't fret, don't go blamin yerself," was Samuel's reassuring reply. *"People can be hard to read at the best of times. They don't always say what they mean especially women. If they tell ye, they're fine, it can mean either they're fine or it can mean they're not fine! Sometimes, you've got to dig a little deeper."*

"You know Samuel. I think you're right. I can just tell that something's wrong. I can't pin it down how I know but my heart tells me something's not right."

"Then, you need to go to her son," said the old sage wisely. *In fact, I think that it's not only Amelia who needs you. I think there may be something to that garden dream you had. I think it means that maybe, a lot of people need you right now because they're being choked to death by the malicious murderous weeds in their garden, the same ones that drove you out, the same ones that are gonna destroy and drive out everything that's good and true in the garden that was once your home.*

I think it's time for you to make the climb my boy. You've prepared long enough and now, you're ready. You've got all the knowledge you need. You've worked hard. You've got the map and all the right climbing gear. I know you're a sensible lad. You'll be ready to make the climb very soon

David, my son. Just a few more months when the snow starts melting on the mountain tops and the weather's a wee bit warmer, then, you can go."

"But how can I be sure that I'll ever find Soul Mountain?" asked David. *"You said that not everyone can find it even with a map!"*

"Aye, that's true lad. I did say that, but I also said that only someone with a true heart and a pure soul can find it which is why I'm sure that if anyone is gonna find it lad, it's gonna be you. It takes someone really special to find and to climb Soul Mountain. You are that special person son. If anyone can do it, you can. Trust me. I know."

David, touched by these words, rose from his armchair and hugged the old man.

"I can never thank you enough Samuel. Thank you for all your help and all your time. I would never have known what to do if I had not met you!"

"Don't mention it son. You're going to make it......... You're the one."

David shook the old man's hand, grateful tears shining in his beautiful ocean- blue eyes.

He hoped to God that Samuel was right.

Chapter Twenty - Errant Red Eyebrows and Shocking Pink Underpants

After Samuel's pep talk and his warm words of support, David knew he was ready to make the climb.

Before he could make the climb though, David knew he had to see Amelia and to do that, he had to return to England. David knew that Amelia normally stayed in on a Sunday as she worked very hard as a paediatric dietician during the week, and Sunday was her one day of rest as Saturdays were spent doing the housework and shopping. She needed her one day of rest as she was busy, busy, busy all week.

Knowing Amelia was a creature of habit, David knew that she would be at home on a Sunday, so the next morning, he donned his disguise and packed a few things into a small weekend bag after which, he set off for the station.

Now, Edinburgh as you may know can be a bit windy in the winter months and David was having to hold onto his kilt for dear life on this cold December

morning as he made his way to the train station exactly two years after he had arrived there on another cold December morning!

Being a prince, he had no experience of washing his own clothes and had foolishly put his white undies in the washing machine with his bright red football shirt with the result that he was now the proud owner of a dozen pairs of fetching pink vests and underpants! The last thing he needed he decided was for people to get a peep at the shocking pink underpants he concealed beneath his black and green kilt, so he held onto his kilt for dear life as he marched bravely towards the station, his kilt flapping frenetically around his knees in the chilly, blustery December breeze.

David really was a brave man to return to England after the trauma of what had happened in the last couple of years. Many before him had lacked the courage for many..... many..... were the times when people had fled and even emigrated in embarrassment from Great Britain to far flung places on the other side of the world like Australia and New Zealand, never to return because someone had seen their underpants!

But now the valiant, brave, lion-hearted prince David was returning to the land of his birth to rescue his beloved England and his one true love Amelia from the scourge of the evil, sinister, treacherous, cold-blooded Septicus Horrificus!

David knew it wasn't going to be easy, but he was brave, he was grave and no ordinary knave although he did have a bit of a close shave on the train back to London which was rather harrowing but he managed to survive it.... only just!

As David boarded the 9.30am train to London from Edinburgh's main station, he found himself sitting opposite a very serious looking little boy of about nine who was sitting next to a very serious looking woman in a grey suit who had her nose buried in a daily broadsheet newspaper which she was studying very carefully as if her life depended upon it!

The little boy who sat to the right of her by the window had little round spectacles which made him look a bit like a little wise owl. He had a little button nose on which there was a generous sprinkling of freckles, and he was studying David curiously out of the corner of his eye.

David knew exactly why the little boy was staring. He knew that he looked unusual in his kilt, with his big, red, bushy beard and moustache and his big, red, bushy eyebrows, framing his clear blue eyes and he smiled a little out of amusement as he noticed the little boy studying him curiously out of the corner of his big inquisitive sapphire eyes....... until that is......something went very nearly horribly and hideously wrong!

As the train jerked forward, David had a strange sensation that something was not quite right. He felt what he thought was a furry red caterpillar hanging over his left eye! As he reached up to see what it was, he noticed the little boy's eyes grow wider and wider as he let out a huge yelp and frantically, began tugging at the woman's sleeve.

"Mummy, mummy, look! Mummy! That man's eyebrow's falling off! Look Mummy! Look!"

Horrified, David reached up above his eye and he realised with a shock that the little boy was right! His left eyebrow was now dangling precariously above his left eye!

Hurriedly David turned his face towards the window so that the woman couldn't see this disconcerting sight, but he needn't have worried because the woman took not a blind bit of notice. She was too busy reading her paper to look at her little boy or anything else for that matter. Her hair was all scraped back severely in a harsh-looking bun and her head didn't move at all as she responded.

"Mmmmmm........that's nice dear. Very nice.......mmmmmmmm mmmmmmmm," and continued to read the paper.

David felt sorry for the little boy with the self-absorbed mother who couldn't even be bothered to look up or listen, but he was relieved for himself because her nonchalance gave him the time to furtively take out a tube of extra strength glue from his knapsack and re-attach his errant false red eyebrow over his natural black one.

"Phew! That was a close shave!" he thought to himself as quickly but carefully, he glued it back on. After two years of daily donning his disguise, he was getting to be an expert at this by now.

The disappointed little boy sat glumly in his seat for the rest of the journey and David was able to relax having checked that the rest of his disguise was safely in place, the moustache, the beard, the other eyebrow. Yep! Everything was as it should be. Everything was fine.

By the time the train had arrived at Kings Cross station in London five and a half hours later, David had recovered from the shock of the eyebrow incident on the train and headed off, full of excitement, to Amelia's house on the outskirts of London.

He couldn't wait to see her again after all these months. Heart pounding, hands sweating, he arrived at her doorstep full of anticipation, a bouquet of pink roses in his hand but what he saw when he got there made his heart sink for something was different, very different from the last time he had been here, that bitterly cold December morning when he had stood at this very front door and told her *"goodbye."*

The difference hit him straightaway. The pretty bright, white curtains which once filled the window so beautifully now looked dull and drab as if they hadn't been washed for months. The driveway which had always been kept so spotless and clean was now covered in fallen leaves which had slowly withered away to a crisp. The whole house looked as if it were in mourning for some terrible event, some dreadful drama or sad story that had been played out since he had been away.

With a sinking heart, David rang the bell. There was no sound. The bell wasn't working. Everything appeared to be falling apart in this once pretty, suburban house. David knocked on the door, quietly at first and then, when there was no response, he knocked louder and louder still, his desperation increasing with each knock. She had to be in surely. He had come all this way.

This wasn't like Amelia. She was usually so predictable, so dutiful, so reliable. You always knew where you were with her. No sudden shocks or surprises, just gentle, steady, loyal friendship and laughs, lots of laughs. He loved her warm, gentle humour. Perhaps, he shouldn't have just assumed that she would always be there, always be the same.

"Everything changes," he thought sadly, a desolate feeling gnawing away at his heart. *"There is nothing you can count on forever in this world,"* he sighed to himself. Nothing ever stays the same, perhaps not even the gentle, loyal Amelia. He should have called her in advance to check that she would be in. God, he'd been so stupid just expecting her to be there waiting for him as always whenever he returned from his jaunts abroad. He had taken her for granted. He realised that now.

He began to worry. What if.... something had happened to her? What if something had happened and he hadn't been there to help her when she needed him, too wrapped up in his own affairs. She had always been there for him when he needed her even when all else had abandoned him, failed him, left him for dead.

Where was she? He was starting to panic now. The thought that something horrible may have happened to the best friend he ever had threw him into a panic. The horrible, merciless thumping in his heart, the sick feeling in his stomach, the sudden desperate need to be near her and the frightful fear that something may have happened to her led him to experience an epiphany.

At that moment, he realised sitting right there desolately on her doorstep that he loved her! He had loved her all along but had been too foolish to see it!

She had always been just good old Amelia, his old childhood friend who was always there, the girl he had always taken for granted. It hit him like a blow to the stomach, like a fall in the snow, the revelation that he had loved her all his life without ever knowing it and now, perhaps, it was too late. The wind knocked out of him, he sank down into the front doorstep and buried his head in his hands in despair.

David was so wrapped up in his own emotions that he didn't notice the graceful, slender figure with the soft, soundless footsteps coming silently, noiselessly up the path until she was just two feet away.

At that point, he looked up, and there she stood, looking down on him with that same radiant smile that had brightened his days since he was a child.

"Davey, what are you doing here?" she cried, her spirits lifting suddenly; it had been a terrible, few months and it was good to see her old friend!

"I came to see you Amelia," said David leaping to his feet and giving her a joyful hug. "I've missed you!"

"Well, here I am!"

"Let me look at you Melia. It's been so long," David said, stepping back a little so that he could get a good look at her. She smiled up at him, but he was troubled to see that her eyes looked a bit puffy and tired like they had done three years ago when her grandfather had died and wait, were those the beginning of shadows under her beautiful, clear, brown eyes?

Amelia's usually fresh, rosy face looked wan and drawn and there was a deep, desolate sadness in her eyes that he had never seen before, a sadness that even her smile could not disguise.

"Amelia, what's wrong?" asked David in a more sombre tone.

Amelia shook her head dismissively and bit her lip as if trying to conceal some deep, dark wave of emotion that was threatening to burst forth like a river bursting its banks. She looked down and blinked repeatedly as if trying desperately to hide away the threat of emergent tears.

"You'd better come in David," she sighed.

Chapter Twenty-One - Amelia

David could see that Amelia had been crying so he got straight to the point.

"Melia, what's wrong? Tell me. Tell me! You have to tell me."

Amelia put her head in her hands and sighed a deep sigh that came from the very depths of her suffering soul.

"You don't want to know David. You really don't," was her enigmatic reply.

"Yes, I do Amelia. I really do," he responded gently, kneeling before her on the living room carpet as she sat in an old armchair by the door, bearing, as it seemed, the whole weight of the world on her young shoulders.

The kind, gentle tone of David's voice and the earnest look in his eyes had an unwanted effect on Amelia. It had been a long time since anyone had spoken to her so kindly and before she knew it, the tears that she had fought so valiantly to hold back now gushed forward forcefully from her eyes and streamed down her cheeks.

Amelia didn't want David to see her cry. She felt humiliated at this unwitting show of emotion. She had always been the brave girl who held in her tears, the stoic who never let anyone see her cry.

The last time that David had seen her shed tears had been the time when she was six when Septicus had pushed her down into the bushes and she had cut her finger.

"Amelia, tell me what's wrong," David's voice was gentle but more insistent now.

Amelia lifted her head and looked into David's eyes.

"Septicus," she sighed.

"Oh, I should have known," said David bitterly, his voice hardening, *"Go on."*

Amelia told David everything, everything that had been going on since he had been away. A dam had burst in her heart and all her emotions, everything, came gushing out in a sudden, unstoppable, fervent rush.

David's anger mounted steadily as he heard how Septicus had bullied Amelia's father at work, forcing him to work extra hours for very little pay, criticising him, carping at him, bullying him at every turn until the stress of working for the tyrant had broken Wilfred down.

When eventually he tried to leave, Septicus, being the bully that he was, had refused to give him a reference because deep down, he knew that Wilfred was the best worker he would ever have but he hated him for being loyal to the old king and queen. At his age, Wilf knew he didn't have a lot of choices so he bore the bullying as best he could.

" I tried to help him," said Amelia. *" I really did. I told him that I'd support him if the worst came to the worst. I have my job at the clinic but...."*

"But.....?" asked David.

"You know Dad," sighed Amelia, *"always so proud. He wouldn't take a penny from me. It hurt me to see him like that all broken and bowed. He'd always been so strong when I was a child- a hero- a real life.... gardening..... hero!"* she said as she smiled through her tears, trying to make a joke of it even in the darkest of times."

"He was a good man," David said, "He didn't deserve that."

"I know," Amelia replied, *"but once the mayor left, Septicus put his men in all the top places. They became the law makers of the land. They made laws that slowly but surely, took away the rights of the common people. Employers could ask for references, but employees had no rights to ask for anything, no matter how good they were and if they ever dared to complain, they'd never get a job again because somehow, somewhere, their name would be put on a blacklist. Dad didn't even have the right to see what Septicus was writing about him behind his back every time he tried to get a new job and funnily enough, he never did get another one, no matter how well he'd worked, no matter how hard he tried. He had to stay at that awful place and be bullied every day until it killed him. His heart gave way from the stress of it all,"* she said flatly.

David listened aghast. *"Amelia, why didn't you tell me all this before?"* All the times I phoned you, all the times we talked. Why didn't you mention a word of this to me?"

"I didn't want to worry you, David. You had your own problems," was Amelia's stoical reply.

For the second time that day, David felt as though he had been punched in the stomach. His old friend had not been able to confide in him while she had always been his confidante. He felt wretched for never realising that something was up. *"My God, she must have thought I was so insensitive he thought. I was so wrapped up in my own problems, I never noticed hers."*

"Amelia, you can tell me anything at any time." he said. *"You can always count on me. I mean, look, how many times have you been there for me when I've needed someone to talk to? How many times have I taken it for granted that you would always be there for me, a true friend in my time of need?"* he asked, gently removing a strand of hair that was sticking to her tear-stained cheek. *"You should have told me, you silly girl,"* he reproached her softly as he held out his arms to envelope her in a big, bear hug.

Amelia didn't resist. She swallowed her pride and held onto him tightly, her tears seeping through his jumper as she sobbed on his shoulder. Quietly, they sat together, arms around one another without a word until finally, the storm died down and Amelia was able to speak again.

From what she told him, David realised just how bad things had been, how, in his absence, things had really gone down. The mayor who had seemed a good sort disappeared suddenly after it was discovered that he was some sort of fluorescent green alien being from outer space, hell-bent on destroying the planet and after that, things had spiralled downwards a long way.

Most of the police no longer did anything to help people and there were whispers that some of them were in the pay of Septicus and his evil friends, that they and other officials were being bribed to turn a blind eye to a dozen misdemeanours every day, misdemeanours that were committed by people working on Septicus and his gang's orders. Others suspected that Septicus and his gang were even planting moles in the police to "take down" the people involved in good policing so that there'd be no one left to hold them to account for anything they did ever again!

Anyone who dared to stand up for the truth soon found that they became the victims of terrible allegations and lies and couldn't get a job for the rest of their life and no one would ever bother to listen to them or look at the facts no matter how hard they tried.

Savage gangs roamed the streets, some in baseball hats and hooded tops and yet others, with university degrees, in smart, snazzy suits and shirts and ties.

Few people got justice in the courts any more for corrupt judges in Septicus's pay could always be bribed and some of the people in the highest places were sympathetic to the criminals because they were secretly, criminals themselves beneath their suits and ties and civilised smiles!

England was in chaos. England was in disarray. Because telling the truth got you into trouble, people learned to keep their heads down and never complain. Everyone smiled for their bosses and for the cameras....through gritted teeth and everything looked peachy clean on the surface until you looked closer and you realised it was a lie. It was all a lie!

David felt as if his heart would break as he heard Amelia's tale of terrible woe.

Now, more than ever, listening to his sweet friend, David saw the wisdom in Samuel's advice. He had learned so much when he had been away. He knew now that he could not fail. He would climb that mountain and he would save lives. He would save his people from becoming a nation of Stepford wives.

David rose to his feet, new determination flooding forcefully into his heart. *"Don't you worry,"* he assured Amelia, *"You're going to see some changes around here before very long. Septicus Horrificus will not be wearing the pants around here for very long Amelia. Just you wait and see!"*

Chapter Twenty-Two - At the Foot of Soul Mountain

In reality, things were worse than even David and Amelia realised. What Amelia told David was just the tip of the iceberg. What Amelia didn't tell David, because she didn't know herself, was that under Morgiana's malevolent influence, the kingdom had become infested with the occult- the menacing, malignant, malevolent kind, the kind that caused people harm.

Anyone who tried to stand up to Morgiana or Septicus or their evil friends found themselves the victims of sudden devastating losses or catastrophes that seemed to come out of nowhere. Some of them lost their health. Others lost their jobs and their wealth and yet others went insane even though they had been perfectly fine before throughout their entire lives!

The evil couple had evil contacts in all kinds of places of trust and had learned that a thousand pounds or two could get almost anyone to do anything they wanted to harm the pesky people who stood in

their way and if that failed, there was always their own peculiar brand of particularly malevolent magic.

It was in this climate that David was making the journey up to the top of the rugged Soul Mountain and it was important that he made the challenging climb, given what his people and his own family were going through.

In the end, it was in April, in the first flush of spring, that David finally made the climb. Daniel and Samuel were there to see him off at the foot of the mountain but before they even got to the mountain, they helped him to check that he had all the right climbing gear as they knew the importance of being well prepared.

Climbing a mountain was a risky business and Samuel wanted to make sure that David had everything he needed to be safe so he could come back to his friends and family in one piece. *"Better to be safe than sorry,"* Samuel had told David several times during the long months they had spent together as teacher and apprentice, and now, here they were, checking that David had everything he needed for a safe climb.

"Hydration pack?" asked Daniel.

"Check!" replied David as Daniel ticked off another thing on the list of essentials for safe and successful mountain climbing.

"Climbing boots?"

"Check!" responded David *"on my feet!"* as Daniel put another tick on the list.

"Suspension harness- ropes and slings- altimeter watch?"

"Check! Check! Check!" confirmed David for the umpteenth time. They went on like this until they had finally gone through the entire list of essentials that Samuel had drawn up carefully the night before.

Finally, it was time to go. It was seven thirty in the morning and both Daniel and Samuel had risen at the crack of dawn to assist David with his endeavours as they both knew that this was a serious mission that David was embarking on...a mission that was going to save his people from slow and steady annihilation by the greedy, grasping Septicus and his evil witch queen.

It was a chilly morning as they stood at the foot of the formidable Soul Mountain. It was always chilly in the mornings until the sun had time to get started with his work and warm the chilly morning air. Daniel and Samuel stood in the cold with a geared-up David, a strange ache pervading their hearts, and warm tears threatening embarrassingly to fall from their eyes.

They had come to care for David over the last couple of years. He had become one of their own. Daniel had always wanted a brother and David had been just that to him over the past twelve months and as for Samuel, well, he felt as if he'd got himself another grandson.

David had had none of the pompousness and arrogance of his cousin, Septicus. In its place, he had a warm and loving heart and it had won him the affection and loyalty of this grandson and granddad who now counted him as one of their own.

So, it was a wrench to let him go alone up the mountain which only a few could find, let alone climb. They knew that the mountain could be treacherous and tough to climb but it had to be done for David to save his people and to get back his life. It was with a heavy but hopeful heart that they hugged the man they had come to love so much and bade him a fond farewell.

"Good luck, my son," said Samuel as he hugged David affectionately, tears welling up for all to see in his wise old blue, grey eyes.

"Take care kidder," said Daniel cheerily as he punched him lightly in the arm and then, not able to help himself any longer, reached out and gave David a hug as warm and as fervent as his grandad's.

"Take care of yourself OK, Davey? We want to see you back on terra firma again before too long son, OK?"

"I will," whispered David, choked with emotion at the kindness and the love that he had found so far away from his home. *"I'll be back with you in no time."*

"Aye well a good prince always keeps his promises," said Samuel so I shall worry no more. God bless you, my son. Come back to us safe and sound,"

.........were the last words that David heard at the foot of Soul Mountain before he began his long and arduous climb to save his people ...and himself. This was the time, the moment he had been preparing for so diligently - for the last two and a half years of his eventful and turbulent life.

146

David remembered Samuel's wise words,

"Beinn Anam can be treacherous at the best of times son. You cannae be too careful. You'll have to push on through wind and through rain- keep your focus through sleet and through snow and you'll have to avoid all the pitfalls and the temptations for they will pull ye down and never let ye up and you'll never reach the top unless ye resist temptation and concentrate on the climb."

David had paid close attention to all that the wise master had taught him. He had listened with rapt attention as the old master taught him about the many tests he would face.

He paid mind to Samuel's talks about the location of the pitfalls and the bogs and the quicksand, all the things that he had to avoid if he were to make it to the top of the mountain. Beinn Anam was not like any other mountain on earth.

It was a special, unusual mountain where a person could expect all kinds of tests and trials and there was no guarantee that he would ever reach the top. If he lost focus, if he allowed himself to be distracted, he knew he could fail but failure was not an option. He could not afford to fail.

As he stood at the foot of the mountain, David knew he was making the climb on which rested his own fate and the fate of his entire nation.

He could NOT fail.

Chapter Twenty-Three - The Long and Arduous Climb

The sage was right. It really was a difficult climb- right from the start.

First, David threw his grappling hook firmly and carefully onto a sturdy-looking ledge on the mountain-side. Then, holding onto the strong, sturdy rope that dangled from it, he did a weight test to make sure that the four prongs of the hook had gripped onto the ledge firmly.

Once he was satisfied that it had gripped firmly, he started to climb slowly, steadily with the utmost concentration. Each time he got up to the hook, he moved it up again and climbed up further, hanging on to the rope for dear life. In this way, he climbed the first 100 metres and then, resting in his harness, he stopped for breath and took a quick sip of refreshing cool water from the hydration pack that Daniel had placed at the front of his bag so that he could reach it with ease.

At this point, something strange happened. As David was taking a sip of water, something came whizzing through the air and bumped him on the side of his head.

Looking to the left of him, he was met by the sight of a particularly, evil seeming troll with malice in his eyes. Soon, another troll joined him and then, another and yet, another, and another and soon, the mountain seemed to be populated with trolls who all seemed to be united in their hatred of him!

"Get the wretched, rotten human!" they cried as together, they lugged mud, sticks, stones and a rather strange, gooey yellow slime at David's feet to try and stop him from getting to the top!

David knew very well that these evil creatures had been sent by the evil and hateful Prince of Trolls who hated humans of all descriptions with all of his malice-filled, stone-cold heart and would do anything.... almost anything...... to stop them from reaching the top of the mountain...... He knew that if any human reached the top of the mountain, they would be saved by the wisdom that lay above the trolls' reach at the pinnacle of the mountain, at the beautiful, rugged mountain top!

It was with reverence that David remembered old Samuel's words, *"When they attack you son, don't attack them back with mud and slime because then, you'll be no better than they are. You'll lose the high ground. You'll slide back down to the bottom of the mountain, and you'll have to start all over again...on the long and arduous climb. A strong man is not just a man who can wrestle. A strong man is a man who can control his anger, a man who doesn't let his anger control him. You must keep focus and control my son if you want to make the climb, if you want to win."*

David remembered all too well Samuel's warning that he would undergo several tests and trials on his journey to the top. He knew that he would be tested on the qualities that make a good king- self- control, compassion, integrity, justice, courage, perseverance, and if he could pass these six tests, with patience and with hard work, he would be rewarded at the top of the mountain with a great gift - the crowning glory of all princely qualities- the gift of wisdom.

This was the first test, and he knew from months of training what he had to do. Quick as a flash, he took out a golden shield from his backpack and held it in front of him. *"Use the shield of truth my son to defend yerself when they attack and above all, keep control. Don't lose your temper or you'll lose your control. Your footing will be strong and you won't go down to their level if you can keep yer head and keep control,"* the old sage had advised him so many times.

The only trouble was that now, they came from both sides of the mountain, twenty angry trolls conspiring against one man, so the shield only protected him on one side, leaving him covered, dripping with slimy, sticky, oozing mud on the other.

David knew, then, that he had to take on plan B which was a special taizer gun made for trolls. The gun was made of clear crystal and was filled with bullets made from Xanthanite globs which the trolls were violently allergic to.

It made them sneeze repeatedly four or five hundred times in a row and it made their eyes and their lips puff up to the size of footballs before making them drop down unconscious at a person's feet.

David knew that the trolls hated Xanthanite as it made them feel very ill, and it would take a long time before the effects would finally wear off.

It was a stun gun for trolls. David reached into his bag and drew out the crystal pistol and he fired swiftly on both sides. David was a good shot for he had practised for months with Samuel on a target board, and soon, the trolls were falling down on both sides, coughing, sneezing and rolling down the hill, yellow smoke hissing furiously as it emerged from noses, throats, eyes and ears.

The few trolls who escaped being hit, seeing the effects of the Xanthanite, took to their heels and fled for their lives!

David sighed a huge sigh of relief. *"Whew! That was a close shave!"* he thought as he wiped his brow wearily with a tissue. Next, he pulled out from his rucksack, a bottle of troll and goblin goo remover so that he could free his feet which were now stuck to the ground. This freed him to move again so that he could continue his climb up the mountain.

The first test over with, David now continued on his way, a little worse for the wear but buoyant nonetheless, as he had kept control and passed the first test, behaving just as Samuel had advised him, *"Thank God! One down, five to go,"* thought David with a weary smile as slowly but surely, he continued upwards on his climb up the formidable mountain.

It was a breezy day. The mountain air was fresh and cool, but David knew that the higher up he got, the colder it would be, so he had made sure that he had dressed in layers. He had learned from Samuel to always be prepared because Samuel, as well as being a sage, in his younger days, had also served as a scoutmaster for his local parish in Edinburgh.

David glanced at his altimeter watch. He was about four hundred metres up now. He decided it was time to stop for a rest, and he took a sip of water from his hydration pack to keep him going.

David stood silently and reverently, breathing in the clean, fresh mountain air. It felt good to be filling his lungs with good, clean, life-giving air. It had been a gruelling climb so far and there were still another four hundred metres to go. He needed this. He really did.

He stood there for a while, catching his breath, drinking in the bracing mountain breeze when suddenly, what was that he could hear? A strange sound -a strangely eery, ethereal sound so ethereal that it sounded like an echo- was coming closer, closer and closer still.

It was faint at first but as he stood there, it began to get louder and louder, - a strange, unearthly hum that began to engulf him as it drew nearer and nearer and nearer still. David closed his eyes for a moment, listening intently to the sound. What in heaven's name was it?

He felt a rush of fragrant, perfumed air, and he opened his eyes to be greeted by the sight of a dozen unearthly sylphs gathering around him, gliding gracefully towards him, fixing him with their eyes, beautiful, glassy, unearthly violet eyes which held him fast with their mesmerising, hypnotic gaze.

These women were exquisitely beautiful, unearthly, ethereal, unlike any woman he had ever seen in his life before. Their beautiful, radiant faces seemed to glow with an inner light, their long, wavy tresses lifted lightly by the pleasant breeze were dancing delicately around them, adding to their ethereal, unearthly, other-worldly appeal.

Eyes shining, their heart shaped faces glowing, ruby red lips parted they came to him as if expecting..... a kiss.

"David! David!" they whispered in soft, soothing, honeyed tones that washed over him like a cool, refreshing mountain breeze, *"Come with us. David. This way. This way."*

Their graceful, slender arms were covered in fine silver bracelets with tiny silver bells which jingled and tinkled in the breeze and added to their hypnotic siren song. Slowly, softly, seductively, they came beckoning to David to walk *"this way, turn this way, come with me...... follow me...... come.... come..... come..... with me....."*

David felt his knees weaken as they fixed him with their mesmerising crystal eyes in which now shone all the glorious colours of the rainbow. *"Come with us David darling,"* they urged him in hypnotic honeyed tones. Slowly, as if in a trance, David began to follow... one step...

two steps.... three steps.... four..... until suddenly, it happened.

The ground itself seemed to tremble and shake as if about to give way beneath his feet. David clung on to the rock surface for dear life. A cracking sound assaulted his ears, and a piece of falling slate from the rock above falling onto this head - snapped him out of his trance.

It was then that David remembered Samuel's warning words about the mountain sylphs, the scheming, wily creatures who appeared as angels of light that hid deceitful hearts beneath their soft caresses and entrancing eyes.

"Oh my God, how could I have been so stupid?" he thought to himself for he knew that in spite of their hypnotic, honeyed tones, they were leading him into a trap.

"Look away.......must look away," he muttered to himself, *"mustn't look into their eyes, their mesmerising eyes that drag men in to drown. Look away. Look away. Look away,"* he chanted to himself, and with dogged determination, he turned away from the unearthly, ethereal looking beauties that encircled him, and he began, once again, to climb.

As he did so, the sylph's honeyed tones turned to shrieks of fury and rage, and the eyes which had been so soft and seductive just moments ago were now filled with hostility, glaring with hate.

Desperately, desperately, they reached for him, grasped at him, clawed at him with their long scarlet and silver nails, furious that he was getting away but as long as he did not turn to look at them, as long as he resisted the temptation to look into their eyes, David knew that he was safe, that there was nothing they could do to him, no way that they could stop him from continuing upward on his mission to climb.

"Phew! That was a close shave..... another one!" thought David thankfully as steadily, determinedly, he continued to scale the mount.

It was a few hours before David stopped again because following his experience with the furies or rather sylphs, he had become all the more determined to get to the top of the mountain as fast as he safely could. He knew that all the tests and trials were sent to stop him from ever reaching the top and he knew how important it was that he did.

So, he had pushed on doggedly for the last three hours not stopping for a break… until now. He had passed the test of control; he had controlled his anger and had not gone down to the low level of the vicious mountain trolls. He had controlled himself with the mountain sylphs, refusing to let them lead him astray and distract him from his mission.

Now, he knew that there would be further tests but in what form they would appear he did not know.

Looking to the left of him, he could see what looked like a crevice in the side of the mountain. Looking more closely, he found that, it was more of a cave. At last, he had found a place where he could stop and rest… if only for a while. He crawled into the cave and laying his lightweight sleeping mat on the floor, David sank down wearily onto the ground.

It felt good to give his legs a well-earned rest. He leaned against the wall of the cave and took out a sandwich. It was satisfying to tuck into solid food and to feel it filling up the hole in his stomach after hours and hours of laborious climbing.

David breathed in deeply and sat there for a while, appreciating the chance to have a rest and recuperate a little before it was time to move on once more.

While chewing thoughtfully on his sandwich, he noticed something in the corner of his eye.

Something was moving near the mouth of the cave. Instinctively, he reached for his gun, ready to defend himself if it was necessary but his fears were relieved when the shadow moving on the wall turned out to be that of a wretched-looking, little mountain goat.

David jumped at first as he spotted a shadowy figure in the corner of his eye but seeing the wretched state of the goat, his wariness turned to compassion as he took in its lean and pitiful state.

The animal was so thin and so fragile that its bones were protruding and it was so pitifully undernourished that its fur had fallen off in clumps leaving patches of bare, pink skin.

Perhaps, because of this lack of fur in places, the mountain goat shivered from time to time as if assaulted by the bracing chill of the mountain air. Despite its emaciated state, David could see that the dainty, little baby goat was quite beautiful with its elegant, slender neck and delicately-shaped head in which there were two of the biggest, blackest eyes which looked at him mournfully as he nibbled on the second of his home-made sandwiches.

David was filled with pity as he studied the nervous-looking, fragile little thing that was watching him warily from a distance, its delicate head turned ponderously to one side, and hungry though he was himself, he tore off a piece of his sandwich and tossed it gently towards the animal.

Slowly, shyly, the little goat moved forward and studied the thing that lay before it on the ground. Curiously, it sniffed the sandwich and then, satisfied that it was nothing harmful, it withdrew with it to the mouth of the cave and swallowed the morsel before retreating, having thanked David with a soft look from its grateful eyes.

David walked towards the mouth of the cave and looked out, expecting to see the mountain goat retreating into the distance but to his surprise, it had vanished entirely from sight.

"Hmmmm....strange......," he thought as he sat back down on the mat after coming back into the cave for another ten minutes rest before he pushed on again.

Looking at his watch, he could see that he was 500 metres up the mountain- only another 300 metres to go. *"God, it can't come fast enough,"* thought David as he sighed wearily to himself and leaned back, exhausted, against the wall.

While resting in the cave, David reminded himself of why he was making this arduous, lonely climb- and as he did so, all the things that mattered to him most crowded into his tired mind. He could picture all the people who mattered to him in his mind's eye: his mother- the queen; his father- the king; the sagely Samuel with his wise eyes and Daniel with his cheeky smile and then, of course there was Amelia....there was always Amelia. Those soft, kind brown eyes, that compassionate, warm smile were the things most precious to him in the world. He couldn't bear to see that smile ravaged through years of suffering, those eyes filling up with tears.

Exhausted though he was, the thought of the people precious to him, the things that he was fighting to save, gave him the strength he needed to carry on.

After about ten minutes of rest and quiet contemplation, David decided to be on his way. He packed up his mat and his hydration pack as well as the plastic food bag in which he'd wrapped his sandwiches and made his way slowly out of the cave.

The fresh mountain air assaulted his senses as he emerged from the cave and his face began to redden again in the cool mountain air. He wished that he had something that could warm his nose!

He had sturdy sensible mountain boots on, a fleece and a good pair of gloves but there was nothing he could do about the chill on his nose! *"Rudolph, the red nosed reindeer would have nothing on me,"* he thought as he began once again to climb.

The strange thing was that this time, the climb did not feel so hard. It was quite curious thought David that this should be the case because usually, the higher up mountaineers got, the longer they'd spent climbing, the more tired they got but Soul Mountain was different.

Samuel was right – there was something different about this mountain. It seemed the higher up you got, the more tests you passed, it became easier and easier to keep going. Samuel had warned him that if he had failed the tests, he would have lost ground very fast and it would have been much harder for him to climb back up, although in some cases with a lot of effort, it could be done.

Still, it was far better to prepare well and pass the tests than to fall and have to get back up again as such a thing could exhaust a man after a while.

Feeling more buoyant now than ever, David continued to climb. He had not gone more than a hundred metres before he came upon a ledge on the mountain. Just to the right of him, he saw a large piece of the mountain that had strangely jutted out to the side, leaving a strange-looking ledge at the side of the mountain.

Looking up, he could see that about another twenty metres up, there was another ledge much the same but a little to the left of the first ledge.

David continued doggedly up the mountain until he was level with the second ledge which was just to the right of him. David looked up, meaning to continue with his climb but then, his eye was caught by something which appeared to be moving towards him on the right side.

David glanced quickly to the side, ready to pull out the pistol in his knapsack if needed but he stayed his hand as he saw another climber coming round the side of the mountain. He watched the climber warily through the corner of his eye.

"Hey there! How's it going?" shouted the man cheerily. *"Havin' a good time?"*

"Hardly," replied David. *"It's hard work!"*

"Yes, it is," agreed the man, *"for woossies like you!"*

David was shocked at the rudeness of the man and decided to ignore him hereafter.

"Grow up!" was his parting shot as he continued to ascend, ever ready to pull his pistol out of his knapsack if the man tried anything.

Just at that moment, there was a sudden gust of wind which lifted David's kilt right up to reveal a pair of bright pink underpants.

"Oh no!" thought David, *"that's just what I need with this wally on my trail!"*

David worst fears were confirmed when the immature man who had now come up to his level bellowed with laughter!

"Oh my God! I should have known a woossie like you would be wearing pink panties!" he teased. *"You really are a wally in yer pink girlie panties!"*

Now, normally, a mountain climber would have worn thick, warm pants but thanks to Morgiana's malevolent magic, poor David had no choice but to wear a kilt as he scaled the mammoth mountain. David was furious at the irritating man and his insulting comments but he remembered Samuel's comment that he should always try to keep his cool.

"Oh, get a life you sad man- find something better to do than going around, looking at people's underpants!" was his only reply as he distanced himself from the wally to the right of him and continued to climb.

At that point, he noticed that out of nowhere, there appeared another climber coming around the same side of the mountain! What on earth was going on David wondered. He was doing so well until now on his own without any distractions. This was not what he needed right now.

This new man who was further down from David and the first man (who David had named Wally in his mind), seemed a lot more mature than the sneering, offensive twit beside him and shouted a simple *"Hullo!"* up to the other two climbers who were climbing up the rock surface above him. He didn't seem as if he'd be any trouble but still, David decided to distance himself from the two other climbers in case they had any funny ideas.

Just as he was about to do this, a piece of slate fell from under Wally's feet. Wally didn't do anything on purpose. It just happened. Soul Mountain didn't seem to like him very much and had started crumbling a bit beneath his feet. A piece of slate fell onto the other climber's head and bounced off it to hit the side of the mountain before making its way down and further down as the wind buffeted it clumsily from rock to rock.

Wally, being the wally that he was, found this very funny and burst out laughing at the second climber's discomfiture. At this, the second climber became angry and assumed that Wally was the deliberate cause of the bump on his head. He was furious and began cursing at Wally, threatening to sue him, have him arrested and thrown in jail as a threat to health and safety!

David was secretly satisfied when he saw Wally being scolded this way and thought for a moment how funny it would be if the enraged second climber were to drag Wally through the courts and have him locked away for being a public health and safety hazard but it was only for a moment because David, despite his anger, was essentially, an honest man and a fair one too.

So, when the second climber asked him to confirm that Wally had indeed injured him on purpose, David told him honestly what he had seen, that it had, in fact, been just an accident.

However furious he was with that irritating twit of a man, he would not tell a malicious lie to condemn him for something he hadn't done because at heart, David was a decent man. He would not lie even about the people who had annoyed him! Even if he couldn't stand someone, he would still be fair to them.

The strange thing about this though was that just as he had done this, a surprising change came over the two other climbers and they looked at each other and smiled, a strange, oddly knowing smile as if he had just confirmed something that they had known all along.

David saw the look and was mystified but he knew he didn't have time to waste as time was pushing on, so he distanced himself again from the strange men just to be on the safe side, and the next time, he looked around, they had both.... disappeared.

David breathed a sigh of relief. *"These things are sent to try us,"* he thought. *"I have to get on."* From a quick glance at his altimeter watch, he could see that he was just a hundred metres now from the top of the mountain. His heart began to beat faster in excitement as he came closer and ever closer towards his goal.

So much had happened since he had started climbing the mountain in the morning. Lower down the mountain, sylphs and trolls had conspired to stop him from reaching the top, harassing him, trying to distract him, hell-bent on stopping him from going where they could never go- to the mountain-top on which lay the secret to eternal deliverance from the evil ones of the world- Septicus and Morgiana and their kind. Then, there had been the encounter with the little mountain goat and the two men who had appeared out of nowhere all of a sudden on the mountain.

It had been a tough climb. Samuel had told him that it would be tough. He had warned David that good things rarely come easy. They take patience. They take time and work, hard work.

More doggedly than ever now, David continued to climb. He was nearly there now after all the heartache and the pain.

David's heart lifted as he began to think of seeing his family and his friends again. The long and arduous climb would be worth it if he could see them smile again.

Funnily enough, he felt lighter than ever now and the climb felt easier after the incident with the two men as if he had divested himself of some great burden that he had been carrying up the mountain.

He began to realise that this may have been another of the tests that Samuel had warned him about and that he must have passed the test because he had noticed that after every test he passed, he seemed to feel stronger and his step became lighter, helping him on and on towards his final destination.

David realised now that the incident with the goat had also been a test, a test of his compassion. The last incident had tested his integrity and his sense of justice for Samuel had told him that, *"a king must always be fair for his people to be safe."* It all made sense now.

Everything was fitting into place. He had faced the tests of self-control, integrity, justice and compassion.

"Only eighty metres to go now," he thought, his heart thumping in his chest, as he continued to climb, feeling lighter than ever before.

A strange, glimmering light appeared in the distance and as he pushed on forward, the light seemed to grow and grow until it was almost dazzling his eyes. David put his sunglasses over his eyes and continued determinedly upwards and onwards on his all-important, life –saving climb.

Closer and closer, David came to the thing that shone on the top of the mountain and there at the very zenith of the mount it stood, the thing from which emanated the light, a jewel encrusted box of gold in which was housed the gift of precious wisdom. David approached the box which was in the shape of a book and slowly, reverentially, he picked it up in his trembling hands.

Inside this box, the sage had told him, lay the precious wisdom dust that never ran out, the precious wisdom that held all the answers to the most important questions of the universe and above all, in it, lay the key to his freedom and his people's freedom from the bondage of evil that Morgiana and Septicus and others of their kind had wrought upon the world.

It was with great reverence and respect therefore, that David took up this golden box in his hands and held it up to the light and as he did so, an amazing change began to take place.

The sun which, hitherto, had been hiding petulantly behind a moody, menacing, rain- filled cloud came jubilantly bursting through and blazed down its rays in all its glory, enveloping David in its brilliant light of gold!

David stood in silent wonder and awe, revelling in the marvellous miracle that was unfolding before his eyes. It was as if nature herself were crowning him king as he stood there at the top of the mountain, triumphant and weary after his long, hard and courageous climb, holding the wisdom of the world in the palm of his hand.

Looking around him, David saw a wonderful sight, a miraculous change. The gloomy, grey clouds which had hung above him, threatening rain, had now disappeared and in their place were pretty, wispy cotton clouds and a multi-coloured rainbow that decorated miles and miles of pastel blue sky as far as the eye could see...

The mountain, which had been barren before, now, blossomed and burst into life for the slate had transformed into beautiful, lush, life-giving earth which sent forth roots and shoots which grew steadily into flowers and plants and slender, trembling, new-born trees right before his astonished eyes.

The sides of the mountain which had been so grey and barren before now, looked beautiful, covered in pretty, purple mountain heather and little daffodils who bent their heads and swayed here and there, and everywhere all over the newly fertile mountain slopes.

This could never happen on any other mountain but Soul Mountain because Soul Mountain was different from any other mountain. Soul Mountain was special.

David placed the gleaming, golden case carefully in his backpack and closed it securely before taking time to drink in the magnificent mountain-top view for one last, precious time.

"Mission accomplished," he thought to himself joyfully before he began the climb down the mountain with a jubilant heart and a satisfied smile.

Chapter Twenty-Four - The Hero's Return

It was a mission accomplished indeed as David made his way down the mountain in a steady, careful reverse climb.

When he finally got to the foot of the mountain, he found Samuel and Daniel waiting there to meet him at just the right time! They had worked out how long it would take David after all his training to make the descent and the climb. Of course, the wise, old sage had timed it exactly right and had got there just in time!

"You did it my son- you did it!" they cried as they danced around him, full of joy and pride.

"I knew you could do it, my boy! I told you so. Didn't I tell ye? Didna?" shouted an elated Samuel to Daniel as he hugged David, tears pouring unashamedly down his cheeks.

"Aye grandad, he did. He certainly did!" was Daniel's cheery reply, his heart bursting with pride at his friend's achievement and relief at his safe return.

"We're proud of you son," Samuel said more quietly now as he patted David appreciatively on his back. *"It's a braw day since you came back down from the mountain. You brought the sun out with ye, so ye did!"*

As a special thank you to Samuel and Daniel, David reached into the box and took out a handful of the very special wisdom dust contained in the box which he sprinkled over them. He knew from what the sage had told him that the box was a special box because its wisdom never ran out and was always there for anyone who needed it to change their lives.

Samuel and Daniel, for their part, relieved at David's safe return, treated him to a slap up meal at the rather swish restaurant at which Daniel had once been a chef some years ago before his change of career to something a little less stressful than cooking for a hundred and fifty covers a night!

At the meal, David asked the sage about the tests which had never happened. What had happened to the tests of perseverance and courage? He was gratified to learn that just by climbing Soul Mountain, he had shown great courage and by reaching the top, he had proved his ability to persevere.

The mystery solved, their tummies filled, and promises made to keep in touch and see each other again, David set off on his way back to London on the train and this time, he was wearing.... trousers!

Having reached the mountain top, having had a taste or rather sprinkling of the wisdom in the box on the night before he set off, the spell had been lifted and he was finally free never to be touched by another spell again!

Now, he would never have to wear another kilt again if he didn't want to because, for the first time in almost three years, he found that he could wear pants! They stayed up! They didn't fall down anymore, thank God!

It was an amazing feeling after all these years of freezing knees and funny looks from people! There were no funny looks from people on the train this time as he returned home in triumph, dressed in a shirt and trousers!

David had decided to keep his disguise on though for the time being though as he didn't want people to recognise him just yet. He didn't fancy being ogled at on the train by curious passengers elbowing each other and whispering excitedly behind their hands.

He had got used to being anonymous during his time in Scotland and he wanted to enjoy that freedom for just a little bit longer until he was ready to announce to the world what had gone on and exactly what he had endured while in exile for the past two and a half years.

The only look that David got this time on his journey home was the occasional odd look from a travel-weary passenger, looking up from his newspaper, curious at the permanent smile on the face of the red- headed man by the window with the curious twinkle in his ocean blue eyes.

Chapter Twenty-Five - It's Not Easy Being Green

Meanwhile, as Prince David was heading home, restored- to his former pant-wearing glory –Mayor Morris was languishing listlessly in an attic room of a small, white house, situated in the furthest reaches of the Outer Hebrides.

Following his impromptu escape from the beach, Letty had suggested they make their way to Uncle Angus's house in the Hebrides away from prying eyes and awkward questions. Angus was her uncle on her mother's side and she had often spent summers here as a little girl so it was to Angus that they both turned when things took a turn for the worse in their own lives.

Uncle Angus was a sturdy old man of eighty five, made strong by years of eating good, healthy, hearty, home-cooked food and a solid, hearty breakfast of health giving porridge oats every morning before he went to open up his little corner shop on the outskirts of town.

Angus had had five boys with his late wife, Elsie, and he had always regretted not having a wee girl to complete the family. He would have loved a little girl to make a difference in a house that had been filled with his noisy, messy, boisterous boys and so, it was with great excitement that Angus had accepted Letty's request that she and her husband Norris or Boris or Morris or somebody or other be allowed to come and stay for a while.

Angus had always had a soft spot for little flame-haired Letty, his little sister Betty's wee girl. Aye, she was a bonny lass who used to spend a summer here and there with her mother with she was a wee thing at her Uncle Angus's house.

Letty was considerably younger than his own boys. His youngest, Billy was now forty-five and little Letty would now be about thirty-nine.

He remembered with a nostalgic smile how the boys used to tease the wee girl when she would come to stay but little Letty was always a fiery feisty little thing, and she could always give as good as she got! If they hid her slippers and pulled her pig tails, she would mess up their beds and put porridge in their shoes and on their heads as they snoozed in front of the TV after a loud and lairy night out on the town!

Aye she was a lovely girl, fierce but loving and loyal too if you were good to her. If you won her heart, she would be the kindest little girl in the world to you. He remembered little Letty with a lot of love and affection for she had always been the little girl he had always wished for and had never had!

So, when she asked if she could come and stay for a while, Angus, without a moment's hesitation, had said a very definite, "Yes!"

On arriving, Letty had poured her heart out to her uncle, and Uncle Angus immediately knew what to do. He offered Letty and Morris his recently refurbished attic room and offered Letty a job in his corner shop as he was getting on a bit now and could do with another person to help him out in the shop.

And so it was that Letty found herself a job in exile in her old Uncle Angus's shop. Being a publicity-shy person, she had never been in the media much except for that one occasion when the press had asked to see her husband's bottom and so, most people did not know what she looked like, especially, here in the outer reaches of the back of beyond.

Just to be on the safe side though, she dyed her hair a mousey brown and wore thick- rimmed tortoiseshell glasses that made her look a bit like Deirdre from Coronation Street or perhaps, a very ponderous and thoughtful, emerald-eyed owl.

While Letty was slaving away behind the counter in Uncle Angus's shop, Morris remained at home in the attic room that he and his Letty now shared. Both Uncle Angus and Letty had agreed that it would be best if he stayed indoors and out of sight.

With his now pea-green skin, contrasting sharply with his shock of very blond and dynamic hair, they knew that he would draw unwanted and unkind attention everywhere he went so they had decided that he should stay safely inside during the day.

And so, lost and lonely, in exile far from home, the good mayor of London, Morris Ronson languished dolefully in an attic room in the far, far reaches of the Outer Hebrides.

Every day, it was the same old routine. The once active and enthusiastic mayor was now reduced to sitting at home all day, mournfully listening to the same tired old tunes on Uncle Angus's CD player, "There Can be Miracles When you Believe," and "It's not Easy Being Green," while warm tears wended their way down his pea-green cheeks and plopped gently down onto the ground beside his glowing, pea-green feet.

It was a pitiful sight as night and day, Mayor Morris thought of all the wonderful things he had done as mayor and all the wonderful things he could have done and would have done if he hadn't been visited by the horrible humiliations and terrible tragedies that had dogged him in recent years since Septicus Horrificus had taken over the land.

All he could do now was listen to the radio religiously every day for news of his beloved London and hope and pray- pray for a miracle to deliver him and his Letty from this pitiful state back to their home in London where they both belonged.

Chapter Twenty-Six - David's Home-coming

Mayor Morris didn't know it, but his prayers were about to be answered because as David made his way back to London, he knew one thing for sure. He knew that Septicus Horrificus was on his way out.... and would not be on the throne for much longer. After years of preparing for this moment, he knew exactly what to do but.... there was someone he needed to see first.

Amelia was overjoyed to see David back on her doorstep........in pants! She could tell from the confident look in his eyes that the climb had gone well and that he was back to his old self. No, he was better than his old self because there was something different about her David now- something better than before.

The boy she had loved all her life had grown up and become a man. Elated, she rushed out of the door to greet him with a hug.

"Davey, you look amazing! Let me look at you. Let me....... look at your.... PANTS! Oh, it's amazing. I knew you could do it! I knew you could! Come in! Come in!"

David stepped into her front room and noted with satisfaction that the curtains looked a lot brighter now than the last time he'd been here, and that the brightness of the drapes was matched by the brightness of Amelia's smile.

Hope had returned with David's promise and that hopeful light in her eyes and the brightness of her smile gave David more joy at that moment than all the gold and silver in the world.

"So, tell me everything Davey. I want to hear everything about your amazing adventure. Tell me all about it. I want to know what happened on the mysterious mountain!"

"I'll tell you everything Amelia, in good time" David promised, *"but I've got to get the king and queen out of that asylum first and when you're all together in one place, I'll tell you everything. OK?"*

Amelia agreed with David that this was a wise course of action and arranged for a visit to the asylum as soon as possible. True to her word, Amelia had been keeping an eye on David's parents for him, visiting them regularly, taking food and supplies for them which were checked by the guards who knew the kind-eyed, pretty, brunette very well by now so when they saw her again for the umpteenth time, they were not surprised.

David was horrified by the wretched conditions that his mother and father had been living in for so long. The room was small and dingy. The paint was peeling off the walls and as he entered, something furry scuttled across the floor. He shuddered to see what his parents had been reduced to but that wasn't all. More horrors were in store for David when he came face to face with his parents because neither of them appeared to recognise him and their behaviour was very strange.

"Hello young man," said his father extending his hand, *"How do you do?"*

"I'm fine. Thank you, sir," replied David, stunned at the change in his father. It was as if he were someone else. *"What have they done with my father?"* was David's first thought. The man before him looked like his father apart from the moustache and the long, shaggy beard that had grown gradually over the past two years. The man's voice sounded like his father's voice, but his manner and his words were not like his father's manners and words at all.

"Young man," said the king, *"You look familiar. Something about you looks familiar.....the hair, the eyes......I know you from somewhere don't I? Let me see........hmmmm...."*

David's heart leapt up at these words but soon sank as the king continued...

"I know! You're Horatio's boy, aren't you? Yes, yes I recognise you by those teeth. They stick out a mile- just like your father's!"

David touched his mouth self-consciously. No one had ever told him that his teeth stuck out before. He looked at Amelia, standing behind his father who shook her head and mouthed,

"Pay him no mind. He's not well."

David could tell that something was wrong with his father because it wasn't like him to make such rude comments about a person's appearance! The king had always taught David very sensibly that it was not proper or nice to judge a person by their personal appearance and had taught him to have manners but now, his father appeared to be behaving very differently to his usual sensible self.

"How's your father young man?" continued David's father, *"Is he well? I haven't seen him in years. Give him my regards, will you? There's a good boy!"*

David promised his father that he would tell his father that his father had sent his regards! It was all very confusing, and David's heart ached to see his father, the king, in such a confused condition, he who had once been so majestic and so strong.

He turned to his mother who was gesturing wildly to him to *"Come over here child! Come here! I want to tell you a secret."*

David went over to his mother who drew him close and whispered in his ear,

"Young man, I need your help. I need you to call the police immediately. That man.... that man you see over there is an impostor. He says that he is my husband, Nigel, but he is NOT! He is my husband's wicked, villainous cousin, Hezekiah and he's come here to ... fizzle my fingers and twizzle my toes! He thinks I don't know but I know! I know .... and the rat knows!" she said pointing furtively to the curious little mouse that was peeping its head out of a little crack that was its hidey hole in the wall.

David knelt down in front of his mother and looked up into that dear, sweet face with tenderness in his eyes. *"Poor mother, if she could see herself now,"* he thought sadly, filled with pity at the life that his poor mother and father had been forced to lead for the last two and a half years since he had been away.

He sighed a deep sigh, thinking of what they must have been through all these years and then, his sadness turned to resolve as he reached into his rucksack and pulled out the precious golden case that had never left his side since his return from Soul Mountain.

Tenderly, very tenderly, he kissed his mother on the top of her silvery white head and then, opening the case carefully, he pulled out the precious wisdom dust which he sprinkled over his mother who was looking at him quizzically, shrinking back slightly, a strange, anxious fear in her eyes.

However, that look soon turned to recognition as the wisdom dust took its effect and her eyes which, so fearful just a moment ago, began to fill with the deepest, profoundest joy.

"David! Oh David! My own dear, sweet, darling boy!" she cried, clasping him to her bosom. *"Oh, it's my own dear sweet little boy!"*

"Mother, mother, please, you're embarrassing me!" objected David half-seriously but still smiling as he

gestured with his eyes towards Amelia who was trying very hard not to laugh at this amusing sight.

The queen calmed down after a little while, gained her composure and was soon, back to her normal self and then, it was the turn of the king to be delivered.

However, David soon realised that this was going to be a little harder than they had thought as the king was now standing on his head on the other side of the room, flapping his arms as if they were wings, making bird calls with his mouth. *"Coooo! Coooo! Coooo! Quack! quack! Brrrr! Oops!"* trilled the king. David and the queen looked at each other. The queen was mortified. "What on earth is your father doing?" she asked, bewildered.

In all her years together with the king as husband and wife, she had never seen her husband behaving so oddly before. She was perplexed. David put a reassuring hand on his mother's arm and promised her, *"Don't worry mother, I know exactly what to do."*

With confident assurance, David strode over to his father and administered the wisdom dust whereupon the king was swiftly released from Morgiana's terrible spell, his senses returning swiftly.

"What on earth are you all doing upside down?" he enquired in a bewildered voice.

"It's not us whose upside-down father. It's you. Look!" said David, pointing to the clock on the wall. The king realised that it was he who was upside down as the three

people in the room and the numbers on the clock all seemed to be a different way up to himself!

With David's help, he got back on his feet, bewildered at what had just happened.

"What the devil was I doing on my head boy?" asked the king who was usually known for his dignified and distinguished demeanour.

"It's a long story father," replied David. *"I'll tell you everything in the car."*

David soon managed to get the Secret Service to talk in confidence with the head of the asylum to have his father and mother released without delay.

Once they realised that Prince David had not actually been eaten by bears, everything changed for David, and he was given all the assistance that a man could need.

The asylum guards were paid handsomely to say nothing until further notice, and all were sworn to secrecy not to breathe a word of any of this to anyone until Septicus Horrificus and Morgiana could be exposed for the frauds and the tricksters that they were.

On the way to a secret home that the Secret Service had found for the family, David told his parents and Amelia everything- everything that had happened on Soul Mountain and in the intervening years that he had been away.

The queen cried happy tears for her boy, her precious boy who had become a man of such strength and courage and who had gone to such great lengths to rescue his father and her. The king was choked with emotion but hid it as he thought under a cool, " *Grumph! That was nicely done boy!"* while Amelia smiled at the happy sight of the family, reunited safe and sound and in their right minds!

In their new apartments on the edge of town, David and his parents waited while the security services put into place an ingenious plan to catch out Septicus and Morgiana and get proof of their guilt so that they could be properly punished for their horrendous crimes.

An officer named Malcolm got himself a job at the palace as serving staff and managed to leave listening devices or bugs in the parlour. That done, everything that Morgiana and Septicus said could be listened to by officers in the service and recorded if necessary.

It didn't take long for strange facts to surface, and the security services were shocked by the terrible things they began to find as the days and the weeks went on.

It wasn't long before they found out that Morgiana was a high witch who, together with her evil cronies, had ruined the lives of hundreds of people who had even slightly upset her or her friends.

They found out that behind his outer mask of kindness and charm, Septicus was an arrogant, mean-minded, superficial, shallow bully, obsessed with his looks and with putting people down!

They found to their horror as weeks went by that Morgiana and Septicus were two of the most unpleasant people in the world!

The lucky strike finally came one Friday night when Morgiana and Septicus, reminiscing in their parlour over events of recent years, revealed more than they would have ever done if they had known that someone was listening at the door!

For the first time in his life, Septicus was being played at his own game and he didn't have a clue about it yet!

"We've got him!" announced the head of the service proudly one Monday morning as he played back the tape of Septicus and Morgiana's late night conversation to fellow service officers who were chilled to their very bone by what they heard on the tape.......

It had been the end of another fun-filled Friday night for Morgiana and Septicus as they lounged lazily on the sofa after enjoying the seventeenth party they had been to that week.

"If only David and dear old Uncle and Aunty could see us now!" gloated Septic after his fourth glass of champagne.

Morgiana hiccupped a reply.

"David's probably still looking for his trousers somewhere in the Honduras! Ha! Ha! Hic! Ha!"

"Yes, that was a terrible spell you put on him you mean girl!" laughed Septicus as he poured himself a fifth glass.

"What a hilarious hic story! Hic!" added Morgiana, *"Mummy and Daddy in the looney bin and poor David left with no pants on, flashing his underpants to the world!"*

"Yes, I showed him who wears the trousers around here!" sneered Septicus spitefully.

"You!" objected Morgiana. *"Darling you would be nothing without my spells. Nothing I tell you! Hic!"*

"I wouldn't say that my sweet one. After all, I was the one who brought you to the palace. I am the one with royal blood. You, my dear, were just a supermodel when I found you and now, thanks to me my sweet, you are a queen... and not just any queen....queen of all Britain."

Morgiana was a bit annoyed by this remark which she thought was condescending so her voice started to get quite shrill at this point!

"Royal or not Septicus, you would never have been able to shut your precious aunty and uncle away in the asylum and get rid of David if I hadn't purposefully driven your uncle and aunty insane and robbed David of his pants with my powerful magic!"

"Yes, I know Morgiana my love, but I was the one who created the rumours about that irritating do-gooding sanctimonious saint of a mayor, being an alien threat from outer space, hell-bent on destroying the world!" Septicus chuckled heartily at the irony of this. Sometimes, he couldn't help marvelling at his own malice!

"Yes, but I was the one who put the spell on him to make your lies look like the truth when the truth was about to come out MY LOVE!" responded Morgiana *irascibly, her voice getting steadily more shrill. You would be nothing without me Septic baby - admit it!"*

"All right Morgi my love. Let's just say that you and I... need each other. We both made this happen. We make wonderful partners in crime! OK? Let's drink to that!"

Morgiana still looked a little miffed.

"I suppose so," she replied a little sullenly as she lifted her glass to his and indicated her agreement with a loud clink!

The tape stopped playing at this point.

"We've got them!" said the officer in charge. *"Let's get the weasels!"*

It wasn't long before David and his parents, the king and queen, were listening to the tape. The family was horrified. The queen was particularly upset as Septicus was her late sister's only child and she had never thought that he could betray them in such a horrible way. Why- he had lied to them all! He had known that the mayor was innocent all along but all because of a petty personal grudge, he had framed an innocent man and allowed an entire town of people to brand him guilty despite his unquestionable innocence and what that awful boy had done to her David. Oh! It was not to be borne. The boy was a monster. *"My poor sister,"* wept the queen. *"She must be turning in her grave."*

"Don't let him upset you Mother," said David as he enveloped his teary-eyed mother in a warm embrace. *"He's not worth it."*

"How did he turn out to be so evil?" sniffed the queen. *"It doesn't bear thinking about! What a horrible boy."*

"Well, you won't have to think about it much longer my dear," said the king in a quiet, steely voice *"because Septicus Horrificus is not going to be with us for very much longer. He is going to be sorry for what he has done to our family and to the people of this country- very sorry and that is a promise."*

The king always kept his promises, and this instance was no exception. First, word was sent around town about what Septicus and his evil bride had done.

Secondly, trustworthy staff members at the palace were told in secret about what was going on, and on seeing the old king and queen, they were more than a little relieved because behind the public mask he wore, Septicus was a tyrant when at home, but no one had dared to speak out for fear of losing their jobs.

Many were moved to tears on hearing about the royal family's terrible ordeal, being betrayed by one of their own family but all swore to keep quiet about what they knew until the time was right to deliver the coup de grace to Septicus Horrificus and his horrible queen.

"The time is now," said the king unwilling to wait any longer and impatient to rid the kingdom of the culprits. *"I want this wretch to be dealt with immediately. I want everyone to know about his treachery and the wicked things that he has done to king and country. I want this weasel, this worm off the throne right now! Get the security services and the police in to arrest him now! If not, I'll arrest him myself!"*

"Let me do it father." David stepped in. *"Let me be the one to confront Septicus. I have waited for this moment for so long. Let me have the satisfaction of telling him his time's up ...please!"*

Seeing the earnest look in his son's eyes, the king knew not to argue. The boy was right. The boy he thought proudly was a boy no more. In the last two years that he had been away and learned to stand on his own feet, he had become a man, a solid, dependable, strong man. He had always been a good boy. The king felt very proud of his one and only son who had saved his life and who was the most precious thing to him in the world. Let the boy have his moment. This was his moment. He was right. The king gave David the nod to go forward.

"It's time my boy," he said simply as he stood with David and the queen outside the palace doors. The butler smiled delightedly as he let them back into their home from which they had been away for so long. *"It's good to see you again your majesties, your highness,"* he said before walking with them to the parlour door.

Once at the door, they stopped outside while the butler knocked and entered.

"Someone very important to see you sir," he announced a little stiffly.

"What? At this time? It's eight o'clock in the morning man. Send them away. I won't see anyone without an appointment."

"They say it's urgent sir," insisted the butler... *"very urgent... an emergency in fact."*

"Oh, very well then, send them in," replied Septicus irritably, *"if it's so dreadfully important!"*

It was at that point that a rather strange-looking man with an unruly mane of red hair, a russet red moustache and a flame-coloured beard burst in!

Now, Septicus expected people to come in reverently, quietly with their heads bowed, eyes down when they came into the presence of a great king. He was irritated by the buffoon's clumsy entrance and his irritation was apparent in his voice.

"Who the devil are you?" he demanded irascibly, rising swiftly to his feet.

"What, pray tell me, is your name?"

Chapter Twenty-Seven - You can call me Nemesis

As David stood there in his russet wig, wearing his red moustache and beard, Septicus failed utterly to recognise him.

"What is your name?" he asked again snappishly.

"My name is David," replied David slowly and emphatically, *"but YOU..... can call me... NEMESIS!"* he added before pulling off his wig, false eyebrows and beard to reveal his true identity!

Septicus gasped and shrank back in horror, unable to believe his eyes for here was his long-lost cousin David, standing before him.... in PANTS!

"Yes, Septicus it's me, your cousin David who you so conveniently pushed aside to seize the British throne. Well, now, I'm back to take back what's rightfully mine!"

Septicus, for once in his life, was lost for words. He ummed and awed, trying to think of what to say for he had never thought that this day would come. As he tried desperately to think of what to say, his attention

was caught by the sound of boos and jeers which seemed to be coming from outside the window.

Looking through the window, he could see that someone had let a large crowd of people in through the palace gates and the angry crowd had now gathered outside the palace while nervous policemen stood by to ensure that security was maintained and so that no one could make a break from the crowd and get inside.

Looking at the ocean of angry faces outside, Septicus knew his time was up- his hour had come. The people were incensed, now that they knew that Septicus had deceived them. The game was well and truly up, and it was time for Septicus to pay.

"Septic baby, there you are," said Morgiana in honeyed tones as she glided into the room, looking a million dollars in an expensive designer handmade, red-silk dressing gown which contrasted beautifully with the rich glossy blue-black tresses that she was coiling snake-like into a bun at the top of her head.

Her eyes widened when they fell on David, standing there so strong and proud, a complete contrast to the shame-faced, embarrassed, nervous person who had fled with his pants around his ankles less than three years ago.

"Septicus, what is going on?" she enquired, her voice faltering ever so slightly in spite of her otherwise confident air.

"I'll tell you what's going on Morgiana," answered David boldly. *"I have come to take back my palace and my throne- THAT is what is going on!"*

Morgiana stared at Septicus and back at David. She could feel another spell coming on. Another malevolent magic spell was just what she needed she decided to put David into the asylum with his parents.

David knew all too well what Morgiana was capable of and decided it was time to burst her bubble once and for all. *"Oh, don't think you can go back to your book of shadows and get me out of the way again Morgiana because I am immune now to whatever it is you are planning to do.*

I have something now you will never have- something that means that the likes of you can never touch the likes of me with your evil magic again! Go ahead Morgiana, why don't you get your dusty old book of spells out and give it a try? I dare you!"

Morgiana dug her heels in at the challenge. *"Nothing is more powerful than magic,"* she declared. *"Nothing can save you from my magic. I am an all-powerful high witch,"* she proclaimed, *" and I will have you standing on your head and eating bugs in a minute if you dare to try and cross me!"*

"Oh really, Morgiana," replied David, *" I would like to see you try. I'm sure my mother and father, the king and queen, would love to see you try too no doubt."*

Morgiana smirked at this and declared, *"I doubt that very much, seeing as they are incarcerated at present and will continue to be so until the end of their days."*

"I wouldn't be too sure of that," announced the king boldly, entering the room in full royal regalia, followed

closely by the queen, both restored to health and both looking very much like their old majestic, selves.

This time, it was Morgiana's turn to gasp. As they entered the room, her eyes were standing out on stalks. This could not be! This could not be happening she thought frantically. Her magic could never be beaten. Never in all the years that she had practised the dark arts had her magic failed her. What on earth was happening here today? How could these people have broken free? This was impossible!

Still, proud and defiant as ever however, Morgiana refused to accept that she was beaten. Instead, she began to mutter something strange, something convoluted, something incomprehensible under her breath. She began to chant in a strange, eery voice. She was sure her magic would not fail her. She had absolute faith in the power of her evil gift. Something was bound to happen if she turned to her old weapon again in her time of need.

Morgiana was right about something happening. Something did begin to happen, only this time something happened....to Morgiana!

As she began to chant, something fearsome began to happen to her. Morgiana began to shiver, first a little and then, more and more and more. By and by, the shiver turned into a shake until she was shaking most frightfully. She shook and she shook until suddenly, she let out the most blood curdling, piercing scream that reached to the furthest corners of the palace walls and shattered the chandelier that hung above their heads.

Everybody ran for cover as they saw the chandelier shake and fall and then, suddenly, she collapsed down onto the ground and began to shake violently as if she was having a fit.

"Morgiana, Morgiana, my love," cried Septicus, *"Whatever is the matter? What's happening to you, my love? Speak to me. Speak to me now. Look at me!"*

Desperately, he turned her over to look and him and what he saw made his blood curdle for Morgiana was lying there, shaking furiously, her eyes, her once beautiful violet eyes, rolling in her head. It was a terrifying sight and even the cold-blooded Septicus was terrified by what he saw.

"What's happening? What's happening to her?" he asked breathlessly, his body trembling from shock.

"Morgiana is facing her nemesis," replied David calmly. *"All her life, she used witchcraft to get what she wanted regardless of the consequences, regardless of the innocent lives she trampled on and wasted in the process.*

Well, for the all the power she enjoyed through dabbling in the dark arts, there was a price to pay and she is paying that price now and will continue to do so until the end of her days or at least, until she has learnt her lesson."

Septicus was amazed at the change in David. The cool, calm, confident wisdom that seemed to pour out from every pore and every vein terrified Septicus. Something was very different about his cousin, David since the time he spent away. Something had changed.

Septicus began trembling all over at David's revelation and a queer, queasy feeling came over him like a riotous rush.

With the once indomitable, powerful, beautiful Morgiana, his most powerful ally, lying at his feet, Septicus knew that his number was finally up, and true to his selfish nature, now that Morgiana was of no more use to him, his concern was solely for himself. He would have to charm the king and queen he decided and placate his pushover of a cousin to get back into their good books to be accepted by them again but before he could open his mouth, his uncle, the king stepped forward,

"Septicus, Horrificus, Germinicus, I hereby sentence you to lifelong exile in the furthest wastes of the North Pole where you will remain for the rest of your natural life," the king announced at the top of his voice to cheers from the crowd outside the window.

"But Aunty Seraphina......" cried Septicus, stepping forward to appeal to his aunt, the queen but his aunt who had always shown him great love and kindness now turned her face away from him, disgusted by his behaviour. She could not bear to look at him after all he had put her and her family through without a thought for anything but his own selfish greed.

Septicus turned to David. That David had always been a milksop he thought, good little mother's boy, never putting a foot wrong, following the rules, soft to the core. Surely, he would relent and speak for him. He had always been such a soft-hearted pushover. Septicus was sure that David would be the first to speak for him.

But he was wrong for David too had hardened his heart and turned away from him, disgusted as he was by Septicus's selfish, despicable behaviour.

Septicus could not believe what was happening. This had never happened to him before. He had been indulged all his life and made to feel that he could do no wrong. This could not be happening to him, a great and gorgeous prince with excellent fashion sense and fabulous hair!

"But Uncle Nigel, you can't send me to the North Pole," he wailed petulantly, *"there's hardly anybody there! Who will appreciate my hunky, handsome, manly beauty?"*

"I'm sure the polar bears will appreciate it," said one of the women in the crowd below, *"when they have him for breakfast!"*

The entire crowd burst into peals of laughter as they imagined how this might come about and wished fervently for this to happen. After all that the wicked Septicus had put the royal family through and all the people of England, he deserved exactly what was coming to him, they all agreed.

King Nigel was as good as his word, and Septicus was soon shipped off to the North Pole never to be seen or heard from ever again and Morgiana, the once seemingly all-powerful, high witch, ended her days in the asylum for the insane where she had once placed the king and queen in her heartless bid for money, glory and above all, power.

The evil people who had once followed Septicus and Morgiana soon found that they had lost their power and while some of them ended badly like their masters, others regretted the terrible things they had done under their influence and sought sincerely to mend their ways by acquiring some of the precious wisdom that David had brought back with him from Soul Mountain.

Those who were truly repentant and sincere found that they could change their ways, and once they were freed from the evil influence of Septicus and Morgiana, they transformed themselves and their lives.

London blossomed again and crime rates fell to an all-time low as the evil things in society were rooted out or began to change…

Meanwhile, in the North Pole, the polar bears were having a field day. It was a great day for the bear community when Septicus Horrificus arrived. It was of little consequence to them that Septicus was wearing a designer outfit or that his hair was done in the very latest fashion from the greatest coiffeur; they just saw him as a prospective candidate for a very tasty, slap-up dinner.

In fact, the day after he arrived, the polar bears had a great party when Big Poppa Bear, the greatest hunter, famed throughout the North Pole among the bear community for his hunting skills snared a very snooty looking human and beat him down into the snow with his powerful, giant right paw.

Septicus, on seeing the big, boorish bear stomping towards him, had first, tried to run and had, then, reached into his pocket to pull out a huge wad of £50 notes which he offered frantically to the bear. *"Everyone has their price,"* he thought. Everyone could be bought. Surely, he could come to some agreement with this big, surly, burly brute of a bear but to his horror, his money did him no good out here in the North Pole for the bear cared nothing for Septicus or his money. His nose was twitching, and his lips were licking as he thought of the feast that he would have on the flesh and the bones of this irritating human twit who kept waving a wad of green paper under his nose for some odd, unfathomable reason!

Great excitement arose among the polar bear community when they heard of this exciting catch and the little polar bears did their customary pre-feast dance around the captured human before Big Poppa Bear pulled him apart with his bare paws. The little ones whirled excitedly around the unconscious human, singing their usual pre-feast song:

"Yum yum, human scum, fills the hole in a polar bear's tum.

Yum yum, human scum, fills the hole in a polar bear's tum.

Have him baked or have him fried.......

He will leave you satisfied..........

Yum yum human scum, fills the hole in a polar bear's tum!"

The bears' celebratory dance grew faster and faster, quicker and quicker, swifter and swifter until finally they fell upon the prostrate human, lying helpless in the snow, in a furious feeding frenzy until the very last thing that could be seen of Septicus was his limp left leg hanging out of Poppa bear's massive mouth but then, that too finally disappeared down Poppa bear's enormous gorge of a throat and that was the end of the all-powerful, all great, all hunky, all handsome Septicus Horrificus!

As for Morgiana, the last that David or Amelia ever saw of her was in a pitiful little cell in the asylum for the insane. It was strange sight to see the once all powerful, all commanding self-proclaimed queen of England, doing a little hoppety skip jump, skippety hop jump before standing on her head and proclaiming, *"I am the queen of the world. Bow down to me YOU FOOLS!"* to the cockroaches and other bugs that scuttled here, there and everywhere across her tiny, dingy, dreary room.

Chapter Twenty-Eight - A Very Special Royal Wedding...

With the plotters and the schemers out of the way, it was finally time for the nation to celebrate! Word spread very fast about the dastardly, dreadful things that had been done under Septicus's tyrannous reign and people sympathised throughout the land with Prince David and Mayor Morris when they learned how they had been forced out of their own homes into exile because of the evil plots and schemes of the despots who had been recently deposed from the British throne.

When the ugly truth had finally come out, the mayor was wholly exonerated, and he returned home to a triumphant welcome. In the eyes of the people, both he and Prince David were now heroes.

On the mayor's return from exile, he was hoisted onto the shoulders of his London constituents who carried him through Parliament Square singing, *"For he's a jolly good fellow,"* and shouting *"Three cheers for the mayor of London- Hip! Hip! Hip! Hurray! Hip! Hip! Hurray! Hip! Hip! Hurray!"*

Mayor Morris smiled a jubilant smile, relieved that his terrible trials were over and his green skin restored to its usual peachy pink hue after Prince David had sprinkled him with wisdom dust on hearing of his plight.

The entire country rejoiced at the end of Morgiana and Septicus's tyrannical reign and the festivities went on for days, for in addition to the end of tyranny, there was something else that the people had to celebrate after the despots' downfall, something very special .... for there was a very special royal wedding that took place that year in the heart of London Town.

It was a May wedding and the weather held out despite earlier irksome episodes of drizzle and rain. The weather forecasters had consulted with the king and queen about the best day to hold the wedding and they had chosen correctly for they had picked the perfect day. The sun was beaming down brightly as if cheered by this wonderful sight.

Gardens all over England had begun to blossom again. Small green shoots were peeping shyly through the moist and fertile English soil and the daffodils and crocuses were out, vying with each other for attention as they looked stunning in the sunlight.

Elsewhere, fragrant roses began to bloom, and the scent of sweet roses began to fill the warm, spring air. The sun, the flowers and the gentle spring breeze conspired to make this day truly the most perfect day for a very special young couple who were preparing to be together for the rest of their lives.

Crowds lined the streets, desperate to get a glimpse of the heroic young prince and his blushing bride. The queen fretted and fussed around David, making sure his shirt was buttoned and his tie was tied – (at last, the day the queen had waited for so long had come - at last!)- and the king relaxed with his family and friends, making jokes about thinking this day was never going to come and worrying that his firstborn, his one and only born son was going to have to get wed in a skirt!

As David stood with his best man Daniel by his side, he felt a delicious fluttery feeling in his stomach as if a horde of butterflies were excitedly dancing around in there in anticipation of the big event and he felt a little light-headed for a moment or two. *"This is it,"* he thought, his heart pounding like a drum. *"This is one of the most important days of a man's life and I'm finally doing it.....I'm getting married to my best friend. This is real."*

The cathedral was full of smiling, happy people, all waiting for the ceremony to start. David took a quick glance around and smiled. There in the fourth row was a very special person for there stood Samuel, his grey eyes, twinkling, beaming at David as if his heart would burst with joy and there to the left of them was one very cheery looking mayor in a very dapper suit with a very fetching haircut, his flame-haired wife standing proudly by his side!

David turned around and gave them all a big smile and a discreet wave as he waited for the organ to start up and for his bride to walk up the aisle to join him at the font. He didn't have to wait very long because before he knew it, the organist struck up the bridal march and everyone turned around to look at the bride making her way slowly, gracefully up the aisle.

David's heart skipped a beat as he turned to look. In fact, his heart began beating more wildly than it had ever done in his life.

As Amelia came to stand beside him before the vicar and lifted her veil, David's heart felt as if it would burst. Looking into that sweet, honest face with the peaches and cream complexion, those dimples which appeared in her soft, silken cheeks whenever she smiled, looking at those big, brown eyes which shone with happiness, all sadness gone, David knew that he had made the right choice.

This was his best friend, his companion since childhood, someone he knew he could always rely on.

So what if she couldn't remember what an own goal was. So what if she couldn't care less about the offside rule because it was "just a game!"

So what if she'd never turned a cartwheel in her life unlike the Icelandic princess who could do a hundred and sixty five cartwheels in a minute! No one was perfect. He loved her and she loved him, and he didn't care who knew it on this, the proudest day of his life!

The king and queen looked proudly on too, tears filling their eyes, as the two young people who had gone through so much to save them made their way back from the aisle, once the vows had been taken and the minister had pronounced them man and wife.

They looked on proudly as the young couple, so dear to their hearts, walked triumphantly onto the royal balcony as man and wife and waved with dignity and love to the people below from whom there rose a heart-warming cheer as they looked upon the beautiful and loving couple who had won their hearts.

The queen was busy dabbing her eyes and sniffing sentimentally into her rose-scented handkerchief, dreaming of the grandchildren that were to come.

The king was relieved, knowing that someday, with David and Amelia on the throne, the nation would be safe and the sage, well, the sage smiled a contented smile for the sage knew a secret that was quite wonderful.

Samuel knew that in years to come, David would become known as King David, the great because of his fair and kind nature and the gentle Amelia would come to be known as Queen Amelia the good because of her genuine compassion for her people.

He also knew that thanks to David's goodness and his courage, the people of the British Isles were destined to live happily ever after, and princes would NEVER be pant-less... again!

THE END.

Printed in Great Britain
by Amazon

47964143R00118